CW00482101

Kirsten Osbourne

Visit my website at www.kirstenandmorganna.com

Chapter One

Shelby Duncan unpacked the last box of equipment she'd shipped from Minnesota in her new office in Scranton. The office was small, but she didn't care. It would work beautifully for her practice. It was hard to believe she'd finally finished her fellowship and was a board-certified doctor.

When she'd left this town for college over ten years before, she'd been certain she'd never come back, but her mother's best friend's health was failing, and her mother was sure it was because she had a horrible doctor.

Shelby had tried not to give in and move back to Scranton, but if her "Aunt Lydia" was having that much trouble, she needed to be there. Besides, her eldest sister Angela had just had twins, and she wanted to be part of their lives, which meant living back in Scranton.

Two of her old high school friends had become nurses while she was gone, and she had hired both to work with her in her brand-new practice. Both had children, something Shelby truly hoped was on the horizon for her, so that they would split a full day of work. It would be the best of both worlds. They were even sharing a babysitter.

Shelby had gone into family practice, and she was glad she had. She wasn't sure she'd be quite so happy about it on Monday when she opened for the first day, but it was just Saturday, and there was nothing to be unhappy about.

Except babies of course. She was going to be too old for children in a few years, and she didn't want to have to resort to freezing her eggs.

She put the supplies into a cabinet in one of the exam rooms, and stood up, putting her hand at the small of her back. Unpacking boxes didn't do her sciatica any favors.

She moved to the front desk to make certain all the forms were in the correct slots. One of her older sisters, Rachel, was going to be her receptionist. Hopefully, she'd last. Rachel wasn't known for sticking to one job for long. She was too flighty in Shelby's opinion.

As soon as she'd finished all that, she made her way to the house where she'd grown up. She was living there for a month or two as she got her practice off the ground, but then she was getting her own place. She had her own room, but she felt as if she was twelve again, living at home.

Her mother still wanted to know where she would be at all times, which was truly demoralizing. She was a doctor, who had lived on her own for more than ten years, and she was having to answer to her mother about where she was going and when.

Shelby drove home in the old beat up Ford she'd bought just before she'd graduated from the University of Minnesota's Medical School. It worked well enough, but she certainly hoped she could afford something nicer soon.

When she got home, her mother called out to her. "Did you get your office set up?"

Shelby wandered into the kitchen where her mother was fixing supper. "I got the exam rooms set up. I'll be working on my office between patients. The insurance companies are sending people my way."

"And I'm bringing your Aunt Lydia in at ten."

"Don't you want me to just find a doctor for her? I feel strange about treating her."

"No, I don't want you to just find another doctor for her. What are you thinking? I don't trust any of them. What do they have invested in getting her well? You know her and have your whole life. I know you love her like I do."

"All right, Mom." Shelby had a very hard time saying no to her mother about anything. She'd been a single mom for most of Shelby's childhood, and though she'd since married again, she still felt as if she owed her the world.

"And I found something on the internet today," Mom said. "I know you're going to think I'm crazy, but I want you to think about it. Just go to this web address." She pushed a piece of paper at Shelby. "Go look now."

Shelby had no idea what she was supposed to be looking for, but she went into her room, where she kept her laptop. Glancing down at the paper, she typed in the web address. "Matchrimony? What the heck is that?"

As she looked over the website, she understood. There was a psychologist with a PhD in New York City who matched people, not introducing them until they were at the altar. That actually didn't sound like a terrible idea to Shelby. She pursed her lips and picked up her phone to call, knowing if she waited, there was no way she'd ever get up the courage.

"This is Dr. Lachele."

Shelby took a deep breath. "Dr. Lachele. My name is Shelby Duncan and I'm a doctor in Scranton, Pennsylvania. I grew up here, but I moved away for school over a decade ago, and now I'm back to practice medicine. I want children."

"Well, you called the right person! What are you doing tomorrow?"

"Taking a day off from setting up my new practice. What are *you* doing tomorrow?"

"I'm driving to Scranton to meet with Dr. Shelby Duncan. I require a full day of psychological testing before I'll match you with someone. Clear your schedule."

"Let me give you my mother's address. I'm staying with her for the next month or two." Shelby rattled off the address. "It'll probably be better if we don't do the testing here."

"No, I agree with you there. I'll leave early in the morning, and then spend the night in Scranton tomorrow night. We'll use my hotel room, and I'll learn everything about you."

"I'm an open book," Shelby responded, and it was the truth. More than a decade of her life had been devoted to becoming a doctor, and she didn't have any skeletons in the closet. Well, not unless you looked all the way back to high school, and then it wasn't really a skeleton. Just her high school sweetheart who had decided to stay in Scranton when she'd gone to NYU for pre-med.

Who could consider something that ancient a skeleton? While she still thought of Nathan on a daily basis, she was certain she was just ancient history for him.

All those years ago, Nate had planned to go to NYU with her, but two weeks before graduation, his father had a stroke, and his right side was paralyzed. He was no longer able to do the construction work that had been Nate's family's bread and butter for so long.

So, Nate had selflessly agreed to take over the family business, where he'd worked every day since he was old enough to hold a hammer without hurting anyone.

They had planned to write each other weekly, and they'd done a lot of Facetime calls, though all of that had stopped before Christmas break of her sophomore year. It just wasn't the same as being together.

The last she'd heard, he was dating someone, and they seemed very happy. She was happy for him, but not so happy for herself. She'd always wanted to ask about him, but she'd stopped. He didn't need her name dredged up over and over again.

She sighed dramatically. Her bedroom was just the way she'd left it when she'd moved out all those years ago, and there was still a picture of her and Nate at their senior prom. He held her close, and she'd had stars in her eyes.

Shelby picked up the picture and put it face down on the top shelf of her desk. She had no desire to think about Nate any longer. Besides, Dr. Lachele was going to match her to the right man for her.

IT WAS SHORTLY AFTER ten the following morning when the doorbell rang, and Shelby's mother called her name. Shelby was dressed in a pair of jeans and a scrub top because she hadn't taken the time to wash real clothes in a little while.

She went to the door, ready to go, only to find her mother talking to a purple-haired woman with crazy eyes. "You must be Shelby!" the woman said.

Shelby swallowed hard. This woman had a PhD in psychology? Did she get it in a cereal box? "Yes, I'm Shelby."

"I think we'll have you married by the end of next month," the crazy woman said.

So, it *was* Dr. Lachele. Wow. This was going to be more interesting than she'd expected. "It's good to meet you, Dr. Lachele."

"It is good to meet me!" Dr. Lachele said, before throwing her head back and laughing, her purple hair bouncing with the action.

Shelby exchanged a glance with her mother, who seemed mildly amused by the other woman. "Have a good day, Shelby."

"I plan to," Shelby said. She'd learned long before that you didn't have good days by not starting them on the right foot.

Dr. Lachele grew serious and looked at Mom once more. "I'll leave a check for the mailbox damages. I know that kind of mailbox usually costs a couple of hundred to replace. Just fill in the amount."

Shelby looked at her mother again, but her mom just nodded. "No problem. I won't take advantage of you."

"You can't! You'll be seeing me for a wedding soon!" Dr. Lachele laughed again—cackled may have been a better word for it. She amused herself a great deal. Her eyes landed on Shelby. "Don't worry, I'm not certifiable. Not yet anyway. You ready?"

Shelby nodded. "Do you want me to follow you?" Following might be the best answer since the woman seemed to be quite adept at hitting objects that were *not* in motion.

"Oh, no, sugar nipples. You get the full Dr. Lachele experience, which means you get to ride in my SUV."

Shelby nodded, not sure what else to do. Surely, she wouldn't die because they were staying in Scranton. Or maybe she would. "All right," she said cheerfully. "I'll be home tonight, Mom."

Adding that last part made her feel a little safer. Dr. Lachele wouldn't dare do anything dangerous with her mother waiting for her. Or would she?

Shelby got into the older woman's car and buckled her seatbelt securely. Then she looked for the handle. Like most intelligent adults, she knew the handle wouldn't save her in an emergency, but she felt safer holding onto it.

"Where are you staying?" she asked.

"Mohegan in Wilkes-Barre. There's a casino, and I booked us for massages and pedis."

"And we're going to do this deep delve into my life while we're getting massages and pedis?" How could they do that with a massage? They'd be in different rooms!

"We'll work it out. I only need eight hours, and I feel like I can keep you for twelve." Dr. Lachele took the stop sign at the end of her mother's street as a suggestion, and almost hit a trash truck. "I swear they weren't there five seconds ago!"

"Most vehicles do move instead of sitting still!" Shelby said, saying a silent prayer that she wouldn't end up as roadkill.

"Oh, and I made reservations for us at Ruth's Chris Steakhouse there in the hotel. I don't know if you like steak, but I do, and I'll be thrilled to go there."

"Sounds good," Shelby said, wondering what that would cost her. She had some money, but she was trying to save to get her own place. But maybe the man Dr. Lachele matched her with would have his own place. That could work.

Finally, they ended up at the hotel. "We're doing steak for supper. We'll do room service for lunch, and then we have our pedicures at two and our massages at three-thirty. Do you think this is one of those places they make you wear a robe? I hate it when they do that."

"I don't know. I haven't ever been here before."

Dr. Lachele quickly checked in, and the two of them went to the elevator. "We'll order lunch as soon as we get up there. I'm feeling like I need more red meat in my diet. I hope they have a huge burger."

Shelby looked at the older woman for a moment. The last thing she needed was red meat, but Shelby said nothing. She wasn't quite certain how there were so many favorable reviews on Matchrimony's website.

Once they were in the room, Dr. Lachele immediately found the room service menu. After a moment of reading it over, she passed it to Shelby.

"It sounds like we're having a heavy dinner, so I'll get the chef's salad."

Dr. Lachele shook her head. "If that's what you want. Maybe we can find a rabbit to share your lunch."

Shelby shrugged. "As a doctor, I try to practice what I preach."

"I'm a different kind of doctor, and I just try not to preach." Dr. Lachele picked up the room phone and quickly called in their order. "Now, let's talk about you. Tell me about growing up in Scranton."

The psychological testing didn't feel like a psych test at all. Dr. Lachele simply asked questions and made comments. It felt like an easy way to get through everything they needed to talk about.

When the room service came, Shelby put some cash on the table where they ate to pay for her own meal.

Dr. Lachele glared at her. "I'm buying your food while you're with me. If you're just starting a new practice, you have nothing to spare. Trust me, I know."

Shelby nodded and reluctantly put the money back in her purse. "There isn't any to spare today, but there will be soon."

"I know how that goes."

As they ate, they continued talking. Soon, Dr. Lachele realized they were going to be late for their pedicures. "Oh, I haven't had a pedicure in at least two weeks," Dr. Lachele said.

"It's been over ten years for me." Shelby thought for a moment. "Not since right before my senior prom."

"Tell me about your prom."

As they walked through the halls and took the elevator, Shelby answered, telling her about Nate and how they had the whole world figured out at eighteen.

"Most people don't end up with their childhood sweethearts," Dr. Lachele said. "Who was the first guy you dated in college?"

Shelby shook her head. "I've only ever dated Nate. In college, I spent all my time studying because I wanted to get into a good med school. I went to my choice of school, but then it was really hard once I got there. I just never took the time to date. Learning was more important to me."

"What if your Nate had been in college with you? Would you have had time for him?"

Shelby smiled. "I would have because I wouldn't have had to get to know someone all over again. Or find someone to date. I wasn't about to go to all the parties on campus just to meet some alcoholic dud."

"I was the same. Didn't meet my Sam until after college, and I love him with everything in me."

By the end of the day, Shelby felt pampered. The pedicures were amazing. She was a little freaked out when she realized Dr. Lachele had set up a couple's massage for them, but everything else was good.

As Dr. Lachele drove her home, Shelby kept her eyes closed, refusing to panic the whole way. "I think I already have the right man for you. He lives here in Scranton already. I interviewed him two weeks ago."

"Really?" Shelby asked, still not opening her eyes. "What's he like?"

"I think you know my rules about that. If he agrees, do you have a church in mind?"

Shelby shrugged. "I've gone to the same church every day of my life."

"Then text me the name of the church, and I'll see what I can pull together. Find yourself a wedding dress in the meantime."

Stunned, Shelby nodded. "All right."

Chapter Two

Shelby sat at the back of the church where she'd been a member for as long as she could remember. It was strange that she would be marrying here, in the place where she'd gone to Sunday school and experienced so many different dances and youth events.

Dressed in her wedding gown, she sat with her two sisters who were there for moral support. She'd decided not to have anyone stand up with her because she didn't know if her groom—whoever he may be—would have someone, and it would be lopsided. Not that it mattered much.

Now that the day was here, she was more nervous than she ever remembered being. Her mother stepped into the room, smiling at Shelby. "You look amazing!"

Shelby smiled. "Thanks, Mom. I sure hope whomever my groom is agrees with you!"

Mom laughed. "He will. How could he not?" She stepped closer to Shelby. "I wish your dad was here to see you today."

"I have no memories of him. I was only three months old when he passed, but...I wish he was here as well." Her father had died in a training exercise for the Gulf War, and her mother had immediately moved back to Scranton to be near her family and support system.

It seemed strange to miss someone she'd never known. Her father had never even gotten to hold her. As the oldest, Angela had some memories of their father, but neither Rachel nor Shelby had any. Rachel was only a year older than Shelby. It had always seemed to Shelby that they had a complete family, even though they never had a father, which was a testament to how their mother had filled both roles.

They talked quietly, sharing memories of growing up together. "Remember when Rachel snuck out at two in the morning to meet her friends and TP that house across the street?" Angela asked. "I loved seeing Mrs. Wells's look when she was sweeping up the mess they made the next morning. Surprised she wasn't wearing it."

Mrs. Wells's son, Tim, had "dated" Rachel in junior high, and he'd broken up with her by telling all their friends they'd broken up after two days together.

Rachel laughed. "And they called the police and said I'd been there to spray-paint their house, and it was just me. But it was really like ten of my friends. I wouldn't tell on them, but they came in one after the other the following morning all of them admitting it."

Shelby shook her head. "I'm so glad Tim wasn't my first boyfriend."

"Only boyfriend," Angela said.

"That either." Shelby's lips quirked as she thought about Nate, knowing she was giving up on her dream of rekindling her flame with him by marrying.

Dr. Lachele joined them, a moment later, walking into the room, spreading her arms, and yelling, "Boobie bump!"

Rachel and Angela were certain the woman had lost her mind, and it was obvious by the looks on their faces, but after spending an entire day in Dr. Lachele's company, Shelby hurried to hug the older woman.

Dr. Lachele looked at Mom. "You get that mailbox fixed?"

Mom nodded. "Check should clear the bank in a couple of days. My husband did the work, so it didn't cost nearly as much as you thought it would."

"You should have taken him out to dinner on me," Dr. Lachele said. "I'm the one who forced him to fix a mailbox that would have been fine if I hadn't run over the thing." She focused her attention on Shelby, not waiting for a response from Mom. "Well, you nervous?"

"Shaking like a leaf," Shelby responded. "Not sure I can go through with it."

"I promise, this is what you want. He's a good man."

Shelby took a deep breath, feeling a little better at the older woman's words. "Still nervous."

"Well, of course you are! You're promising to have and to hold and cherish and all that other stuff today. But it's the right thing for you to do. Definitely."

"All right. If you say so."

"I do say so! And if you back out, I'm forcing another couple's massage on you."

"No, thank you! One was more than enough." Shelby was still in disbelief over the couple's massage. Who could possibly think that was a good idea?

Dr. Lachele looked at her watch. "It's time.

Mom stood up. "You girls go ahead," she said to Angela and Rachel. "I'm walking my daughter down the aisle."

"I don't mind if Bryan does it if you don't want to!" Shelby said, referring to her step-father.

"No need," Mom said. "I want to walk my baby girl down the aisle."

"You're the best mom ever!" Shelby said. "Thank you for all you did for us over the years." Shelby blinked to hold back tears. She didn't want her mascara to run. No one wanted to look like a raccoon on her wedding day!

During the long walk down the aisle, Shelby's eyes were on her groom. He was facing the pastor, and she was dying to know his appearance. Not that looks mattered to her overly much, but it would be nice to see him.

When her mother placed her hand in his, strong fingers wrapped around hers, and she looked at his face for the first time. At least the first time in this decade. "Nate?" she whispered.

He was obviously as shocked as she was. "Shelby?"

She nodded, and he pulled her into his embrace, right there in front of the congregation gathered for their wedding. "I missed you so much!" she whispered.

The pastor cleared his throat, and though he kept an arm around her, they started the ceremony. When the pastor said, "You may now kiss the bride," it was as if they'd never been apart. His lips against hers had never felt more natural or more perfect.

Walking back down the aisle together as husband and wife made her feel as if she was walking on air. She smiled as she spotted his mother and younger sister. How could marrying someone who was supposed to be a stranger feel so right?

They went to the fellowship hall for the reception, which had been planned as a huge taco bar, with everyone bringing something to add, because there wasn't enough time to find a caterer. Nate had said nothing else since he'd spoken his vows, but his grip on her hand told her he was never letting go.

As she and Nate stepped into the room, he spotted the taco bar and laughed softly. "I guess I shouldn't be surprised. I've never met anyone who was as interested in tacos as you are. It's like every other food is inferior."

She grinned at him. "I've branched out...now I eat burritos, enchiladas, taco pizza..."

He chuckled. "You are the same girl from high school, I'm sure."

She shrugged. "I've grown quite a bit since high school. I have my own medical practice now."

"I'd heard you were in medical school, but no one really knew where."

"No one?" she asked, wondering who all he'd talked to.

"Oh, at the class reunion."

"I see. I went to the University of Minnesota Medical School after finishing up my undergrad at NYU. What about you? What have you been up to?"

He rubbed the back of his neck, which was bright red from his hours in the sun. "I'm still running the family business. Dad died a couple of years ago, but my mother couldn't see the business go under. She feels like it's the last part of Dad that's still alive. So, I ended up taking ten years to get a four-year degree in business, but I feel like it's helping the business a lot."

"I think it's awesome you were able to still get your degree!"

He nodded. "I'm not a CPA. I thought about doing the extra classes, but it's not like I'd have time to do anyone else's taxes. I can do my own, and that's what really matters."

"And maybe mine," she said grinning at him. "I have three employees and patients coming out my ears."

"I'm sure you do! How long have you been back in town?"

"A month and a half? I was getting my office set up when Mom suggested Matchrimony. I guess I should have just looked you up."

He reached out and stroked her cheek. "It may be better it happened this way," he said. "I don't know how I would have reacted after you quit taking my calls."

She frowned. "I quit receiving calls."

He shrugged. "I guess it doesn't matter. I couldn't leave Scranton, and you were busy with medical school."

"That's true. There were a lot of busy, grueling years. I haven't even been back here since right after I graduated from NYU when Mom married Bryan."

"I didn't know you came back then. I kind of asked around and watched for you, but I never saw you."

"I was going to go to your parents' house to see what you were up to, but I heard you were dating Candi."

"We went out twice and called it quits. I never was able to date anyone for long after you."

Dr. Lachele interrupted. "You two need to start mingling instead of standing there yakking at one another. Get some food. I made some nachos from the taco bar, and it was amazing!"

Shelby nodded, walking toward the line for food, aware that she was pulling Nate along as she went. She made a pile of nachos, feeling they would be easier than a taco. As she watched, Nate made himself a couple of burritos. As soon as they sat down with their food, her mother came out of nowhere and tied a towel around her neck. Shelby felt like an idiot, but at least her wedding dress wouldn't be forever tacoed.

As they ate, many people came to visit. Well, not too terribly many because they'd only invited fifty people between them, but enough. His mother and sister both came over to hug her. "I'm so glad I can finally call you daughter," Mary, Nate's mother, said. "It feels like it's been forever."

"I know! It's good to be home."

By the time they left, his car laden with gifts, she was exhausted. "Why does it feel like that took twelve hours?"

He chuckled. "It was only a couple of hours."

"Still...felt like forever to me." As he started driving, she asked, "Where do you live? I've been living with my mom."

"I'm still here in Scranton. I have a house that I bought and remodeled. We'll probably want to sell it soon and do the same. House flipping has added significantly to my income, especially since I live in the house I'm working on."

"Do you still support your mom with the business?" she asked. She didn't mind if he did, but knowing would be good.

"No, not anymore. She gets social security, and Dad put money away for retirement. And I fix anything she needs fixed and am always renovating her house."

"So normal son stuff."

He pulled up in front of a beautiful home. "This is your renovation?"

"It was. I finished it a few months ago, but I didn't want to start a new one during summer. The construction season is always so busy. I have more time during the winter, and I work on the house then."

"You know I'll be working crazy hours, right?"

"I figured you'd have some long days as you're building up your practice. What hours do you think you'll be working?"

Shelby sighed. "Right now I'm going in at eight and leaving at five, but I'm on call in the evenings. I've had a couple of women transfer their prenatal care to me, so I'll be on call to deliver babies as well."

"Are you an Obstetrician?" he asked.

She shook her head. "No, family practice, but so many people come to me with different things. I'm kind of the doctor who will see anyone and everyone."

"Pediatrics?" he asked.

She nodded. "I did a fellowship in pediatrics and another in internal medicine. I'll be seeing anyone who is sick." She shook her head. "Scratch that. I will not see family."

"That makes lots of sense," he said. "All right. Let's go see the house. I'm pretty proud of it." He got her things from the back of his truck, carrying them inside for her. "I'm going to leave these in the entryway while I show you."

"All right." He led her into the kitchen. The marble countertops gleamed, and the tile floor was beautiful. "Who picks the colors for you?" She remembered that he'd never been good at matching anything.

"Maisie," he said, mentioning his sister. "She loves to get involved with my projects, and I refer her to clients as an interior decorator."

"I didn't know she was an interior decorator!"

Nate smiled at her. "There's lots of things you don't know." He led her into the dining room, which had a built-in hutch and a pass-through window to the kitchen.

"This is fabulous!"

"Maisie suggested the hutch and the tile flooring continuing from the kitchen. I would have put carpet in here, but she said to do tile."

"She has really good taste."

"Of course, she does. She picked me for a brother."

Shelby laughed. "I bet it's fun to work with her."

"Sometimes. She'll get an idea of how something should look in her head, and I'll make it exactly like she describes, but it's never quite right. Sometimes I want to shake her." Nate shook his head. "Here is the living room."

It was a large comfortable room with comfortable-looking furniture. Shelby could see her and Nate sitting there after a long day of work, snuggling together as they watched TV. It was something to look forward to.

"Everything is impeccable!"

"Only because Maisie insisted I hire a cleaning service before we married."

Shelby smiled. "We may want to keep that going. Not sure how much time I'll have to actually clean."

"But you'll have time for me, right?"

"Of course!"

Chapter Three

After the house tour, Nate carried Shelby's suitcases upstairs. "I'm assuming you have a lot more to bring over," he said.

She nodded. "Mainly just my computer desk and things like that. My bedroom was kept as a shrine. It looks just the same as it did when I was a teenager."

He chuckled. "Your mom was such an amazing mom. I hope she still loves me as much as she did when we were teenagers."

"Oh, yeah. She was mad that I wouldn't look you up and see if you wanted to go out with me." Shelby rubbed the back of her neck. "Guess I'm still old-fashioned when it comes to asking guys out."

"I prefer to do the asking, but if you'd called...I don't know what I would have done."

"Why did you contact Matchrimony?" she asked, sitting at the foot of his bed.

He shrugged. "I couldn't really get serious about dating after you, and Mom has been on me forever to get married and give her grandbabies. Her health isn't what it was, and I wanted to at least attempt to make her happy. She was ecstatic when she saw it was you I was marrying."

"My mom felt the same, I'm sure. I actually talked about you to Dr. Lachele. I'm surprised she didn't give anything away."

He looked at her, raising one eyebrow. "Oh?"

"You know...she asked about dating history, and I told her about you." Shelby shrugged. He'd broken her heart once, and she didn't know if she wanted him to have the power to do it again.

He moved to sit beside her, looking into her eyes. "I told her about you as well. You were the one who broke my heart by moving away and

18

following your dreams. It's not that I didn't want you to follow your dreams because of course I wanted you to be happy, but that left me here taking care of business."

"I so wish we'd been able to follow our plan. Move to NYU together and then get married after college grad. Then you could go with me while I was in medical school." She looked down at her hands. "I admire you for staying and taking care of your family, but I wish we'd been together at the same time, if that makes any sense at all."

"Of course it does," he said. "When I heard you'd moved to Minnesota, I figured I'd never see you again."

"I liked Minnesota," she said honestly. "I thought about setting up a practice there, but my mom begged and begged me to come back. I couldn't stay away when I thought about all her sacrifices for us."

"Did you ever think about coming back here to be with me?" he asked.

"Honestly, I'd heard you'd moved on. I didn't come home often after leaving for school, but every time I did, someone would tell me you were dating someone else. I didn't think I could call you and mess something up for whoever you were with, so I didn't."

He nodded, looking sad. "I thought about it all the time. The possibility you'd move back here, and our eyes would meet across the room somewhere, and we'd pick up where we left off."

Shelby nodded. "I thought about it too. But I don't want to pick up where we left off. We were teenagers playing at being in love. Now we're adults, and I hope we'll still get along. I can't imagine my life without you, but neither can I imagine you in it. We're going to have to work at getting to know each other again and not just assume we know everything about each other."

He frowned for a minute. "What about sex? I mean, we're married and all. How do we feel about sleeping together?"

She didn't tell him how she'd melted in his arms when he'd kissed her after their wedding. "I think sleeping together is fine. It's part of being married after all." She didn't add that she'd planned to ask whomever she married to wait. What was the point? Marrying him made everything different.

He nodded. "Good. I know we decided to wait til we were married back when we were in high school. But we got married today, and I don't want to keep waiting. Not with you."

"So we'll have a real wedding night tonight," she said, smiling at him. His touch had always made her body go crazy. She wanted to grab him and start kissing him right away, but she knew better. She'd wait.

"Do we have to wait for our wedding *night?*" he asked. "I mean, we're married, and we're alone, and we're sitting here on my bed..."

Her eyes met his and she saw his grin. Oh, how she'd missed it. "Well, I was always told to wait for my wedding *night.*"

He chuckled, gathering her close and kissing her again. He hoped he hadn't misremembered how right everything had felt when he'd kissed her at the church. Surely, he'd mistaken it all. He couldn't let her break his heart all over again.

His kiss sent tingles of feelings through her body, and she couldn't help but succumb to them. She opened her mouth for his kiss and ran her hands over his shoulders, which were much broader than she remembered. He had the body of a weightlifter, but she knew he wasn't a gym rat. No, he worked for a living, and that gave him the body she so appreciated.

His hands began their exploration of her body. In high school, she'd been skinny and flat-chested, but now, she'd filled out, added on ten pounds which made her body even more perfect in his eyes. And her breasts. They'd been forbidden territory back then, but his hand moved to cup one.

She moaned softly against his lips. "We're not waiting for it to be dark, are we?"

"I'm sure not," he replied. Abruptly, he stood up and stripped down to the waist, kicking off his shoes. He still wore the dress pants he'd worn to the wedding, but he could keep them on for a little longer.

He pulled her to her feet and went to work on the million buttons at the back of her dress. "There's a zipper," she told him to make the task easier.

He frowned and then found the hidden zipper behind all the buttons. "You just saved me an hour," he said. "My fingers are much too big for a million buttons."

She laughed. "Wedding dresses need to be easy to get out of."

"This is so much easier than it looked. I feel like I was given a present that required a hammer to get it out of its box. But this is not bad at all!"

When he had her wedding dress dropped to her feet, she stepped out of it, but picked it up to hang immediately. "Are you planning on wearing that again?" he asked, surprised she cared about the dress.

"I was hoping maybe our daughter would want to wear it someday," she responded. "I'm more sentimental than you realize." She had moved very little from home to home, but she had a box of mementos from their relationship.

After the dress was hung, she faced him in just her slip. He'd seen her in a bathing suit a hundred times when they were younger, but this felt so much more intimate.

"You're beautiful," he said softly, his hand going to push down one of the straps of her full slip.

She reached out and touched his bare chest, her hand moving over it and down to his flat stomach. "So are you," she said, grinning.

"Men can't be beautiful, silly."

"I always thought you were."

He shook his head, lowering it to kiss her once more. When his lips touched hers this time, she gave herself over to the sensations he was causing within her. No need for thoughts or anything but how it felt to have his fingers touching her through the thin fabric of the slip.

She wasn't surprised to feel the silky fabric of the slip slide up her body and over her head, and she cooperated as best she could, left before him in only her white silky bra and matching panties.

"You mind if all this comes off too?" he asked, waving to the clothes she was still wearing.

She grinned. "Not if you don't mind all that coming off," she said, waving to his dress slacks and socks.

"I think we can make that happen." He went to work, and in moments, they stood nude in front of one another, something she'd fantasized about since she was younger.

They both stared openly at one another's bodies, the heat between them almost unbearable. Then Nate pushed her down onto her back on the bed, and he followed her down, trailing kisses across her body.

When he joined their bodies together, the passion was so intense for her that she barely noticed the pain. It had been so long that this man had lived in her mind and having him inside her body was something she had known she wanted for years.

She wrapped her legs around his waist, pulling him deeper within her, and she held tightly to his shoulders. It wasn't long before she climaxed, and he quickly joined her, moving to her side so as not to crush her.

He gathered her close, and as their breathing returned to normal, he held her and stroked her body. She was everything he'd dreamed of when he was just a boy, and now, she was everything he needed as an adult. But, he couldn't tell her that, because she would have too much power over him. His heart had to remain intact this time.

They snoozed for a bit, and when she woke, she was hungry. "Feed me!" she said, grinning at him.

He groaned. "I almost forgot how you were always hungry. That hasn't changed?"

She shook her head. "No, and I'm coming off of living on ramen noodles for ten years. I want real food!"

He chuckled. "We could go out or we could DoorDash something."

"I don't want to have to put on real clothes to go anywhere," she said. "I want to wear jammies, so you can go to the door. What's on DoorDash here?" She'd had food delivered a few times to the hospital, and that had gone well for her. She was definitely a fan of all the delivery options that were available.

"Let's do Bravo Tex-Mex," he said.

"Now you're speaking my language."

They both dressed, her in her jammies, and he in shorts and a t-shirt, and they went downstairs. While she looked up what they had at Bravo, he watched her. "What are you looking at?" she finally asked, once she'd decided on enchiladas.

"My wife," Nate said, reaching out and brushing the back of his fingers against her cheek.

She wasn't certain how to respond to that. "I want enchiladas," she told him.

"What kind?"

"Chicken." He picked up his phone and went to the DoorDash app. "Do you cook?"

She shrugged. "About as much as I did when you knew me before. I can make a few things, but I haven't really had time to learn to cook well."

"All right," he said, his fingers punching in their order.

"Do you cook?" she asked.

He smiled. "Actually, I do. I've learned to make a lot of different meals over the years, and I love to grill out."

"I'm going to have to take advantage of that," she said.

"I'm too busy in the summer to do much, but it's already mid-September. I'll be getting slower at work in the next month or two, so then I'll cook for you."

"Good answer!" she grinned at him. "Oh, I took Monday off work. I wasn't sure if I'd need an extra day to get to know my new husband."

"I can take Monday. My assistant can handle the crew."

"Your assistant? You're the big boss man now!"

Nate shook his head, laughing. "I've tripled the size of the company. I try to line up interior jobs for the winter, and I can usually keep everyone busy. My dad built a good company, and we have a great reputation in the community."

"That's wonderful! You'll have to help me with some of the business stuff. I feel completely lost. I mean, I know what the clinic needs, and I'm ordering it, but it feels like I'm really lost with payroll and stuff."

"I can help you set up a system. Who will be doing your payroll?" he asked.

"Rachel. She's my receptionist."

He nodded. "All right. Does she have any college or anything?"

Shelby shook her head. "She doesn't. She's been flitting from one job to another since high school."

"She's not dumb though," he said. He remembered her clearly from high school, where Rachel had been a year ahead of him and Shelby. "I can teach her if she's willing to learn."

"She says she is. She wants to be done changing jobs so often."

"Good," he said. "I'll find some time to run by your office one day this week and work with her."

"She works every day from eight to five."

"Sounds good. You'll have to jot down the address for me."

"I thought getting married would make me think less about work. Here you are offering to help, and I'm very grateful."

"You know I'll help however I can," he said. When the doorbell rang, he stood up. "I'll meet you in the dining room."

She went through the kitchen and grabbed plates and silverware for them, then set the table. When he joined her in the dining room, she was ready. He passed her the food she'd ordered and put chips and salsa in the middle of the table.

While they ate, they chatted about different things they'd done over the past ten years while they'd been apart. "I had a job in college waiting tables," she said. "It was ridiculous. I think I still hold the record for most broken plates."

He laughed. "I've only ever done the one job, but I have worked to grow Dad's business to something he and Mom could be proud of."

"How did he die?" she asked.

"Another stroke. He never would keep his blood pressure under control."

"I'm sure you miss him. Is it strange doing the job he did for so long?"

"In some ways. In others, I feel like I'm doing what I was born to do. I wasn't meant to sit behind a desk. Is it weird that you're married to a blue-collar worker?" he asked.

She shook her head. "Nope. Just weird to be married."

Chapter Four

They spent a lazy Sunday at home, and he made supper for them. She watched him cook, surprised at how very comfortable he was in the kitchen. She'd expected him to eat out most meals, and while they'd ordered in the night before, he said it wasn't his habit at all.

He made shrimp fettuccini alfredo, and it was absolutely delicious. "This alfredo sauce is to die for!" she said as she took her first bite. "Did your mom help you learn?"

He shook his head. "I love the food network. I watch their shows all the time, and they have this cooking course you can take. I enrolled a couple of winters ago, and I still watch to learn new things to cook a lot. If I'm waiting for a doctor or a client, I'll sit and learn to make something new."

"This came from that?"

He nodded. "You could learn to cook that way as well, I think."

"I could if I was inspired to do so. I'm not sure I'm up for any more learning for a little bit. So many years have gone into schooling that I'm ready to give my brain a break."

"That's fair," he said. Nate reached for the parmesan cheese. "I just have to add a little more..."

"When was the last time someone checked your cholesterol?" she asked, as she eyed the shaker. There was a lot of parmesan cheese in the alfredo sauce, and he was adding more?

He shrugged. "I don't think anyone has. Why?"

"When you come to the office this week, I'm doing a full-blood panel on you. Your dad always looked really fit, and he had strokes young. If there's something wrong, I'll find a doctor for you."

"You won't treat me?" he asked, surprised.

"It's unethical. I won't treat any relatives. I feel bad enough treating Mom's best friend."

"Is Aunt Lydia going to be okay?" he asked.

Shelby shrugged. "If she listens and does as she's told, she will be."

"Does it make you crazy when people don't do what they're supposed to do?" he asked.

"More so than I can express. I had a patient at the hospital in Minnesota who had congestive heart failure. I told him over and over that he needed to be careful and not eat so much red meat. And he needed to cut down on his sodium. Every time he came into the ER where I was working, his wife was with him, and he'd tell me he was sticking to his diet and doing everything he should be, and she was sitting behind him shaking her head."

"Did he go to the ER a lot?"

"At least once a month for the years I was in the ER."

"Was he the norm or an aberration?" Nate asked.

"Most people have a hard time eating only what they should. I was just thankful his wife was honest with me, or I'd have thought something was happening inside him to make him worse. I think he gained a hundred pounds in the years I saw him."

"That's really ridiculous," he said.

Shelby nodded. "He made me crazy. Seriously, I didn't know what to do with him after a while. He should have been calling his cardiologist's office when he was having chest pains, not going to the ER. But after hours, they would tell him to come to me, and I would make sure he wasn't having another heart attack and send him home."

"Are you allowed to talk about your patients?"

"If I don't identify them, I can. But say your mom came in to be treated, I couldn't come home and tell you what I'd found out about her."

"That's reasonable," he said.

After supper, she did the dishes. "You cooked, so I'll clean," she said.

He nodded. "Sounds fair to me."

While she cleaned the kitchen, he went into the living room and watched another one of the videos from the cooking school on his phone. With two of them, they should eat at home more often than eating out, and he needed to find easy meals he could do. He liked to cook elaborate meals, but he only cooked when he wanted to. He had a feeling the doctor in Shelby wouldn't approve.

When Shelby joined him, he was still stunned that he was married to the only girl he'd ever loved. He watched her come into the living room and sit down beside him on the couch.

"I'm looking for easy weeknight meals for us. Any thoughts?"

"Crock Pot meals?"

"That's not a bad idea. I could start something in the morning before work, and then we could eat it for supper that night."

"Mom usually starts something the night before, so it'll get super tender while it cooks." Shelby had watched her mother deal with working full time and feeding three growing girls meals for years. Maybe she couldn't cook, but she was good at suggesting things.

"I think that's a good idea, depending on what it is. I could also do all the prep at night and keep it in a baggie to throw in the pot in the morning."

She nodded. "Then you don't necessarily have to get up early to start a meal."

"Do you still hate mornings as much as you always have?" he asked.

She nodded emphatically. "Yes, and I was mostly on nights for the past four years, so...it's worse than ever."

"I'm not going to have to drag you out of bed in the mornings, am I?"

"Probably not. But if you could drag me to bed at night, that would be lovely."

Nate laughed, shaking his head. "I do think we're going to make this work."

"We don't have a choice for the next year," she said. "We both signed a contract that we would stay together for at least a year."

"That's true. I don't see myself looking for a way out though."

"Me neither!"

"You know, we could run to your office tomorrow and talk to Rachel. Did you close the office?"

She shook her head. "The nurses and I have the day off, but Rachel is working, taking appointments and taking calls for prescription refills."

"Did you buy someone else's practice, or are you just starting fresh?" he asked.

"Starting fresh. Dr. Campbell who I saw when I was a kid just retired, and he's sending everyone to me though. It's given me a quick start."

"I remember him. I never saw him as a patient, but I remodeled his kitchen."

"How was he to work with?" Shelby asked. She'd known the man her entire life, and he'd always seemed so laid back.

"Super easy," Nate said. "Though his wife was a bit of a pill."

"Most doctor's wives I've met are like that," she told him. "They figure since they married a doctor, they're better than everyone else. It's tough to be around them."

"Maybe I'll adopt that attitude. I'm the husband of a doctor," he said.

"You might want to keep working while I build my practice up," she said, "but then you can be my trophy husband."

He wrinkled his nose. He didn't care if she made lots more than him, but it did feel a bit weird. He was supposed to be the breadwinner after all. His mother had never worked a day in her life.

"I don't think I'll ever be much of a trophy husband," he said. "I'm more the type to work hard and eventually retire."

"You know I'm just joking. Does it bother you that I'm working?"

"On one level of my brain, I know you've been working for more than ten years to become a doctor, and it's what you've always wanted to do. On another level, I feel like my wife should have the luxury of staying home and raising our kids, just like my mom did."

"The difference is that your mom wanted to stay home and raise kids. And it's great if a woman can do that if that's what she thinks is right for her and her family. It's not right for me. I watched my mom work my whole life, and she still works. She's not ready to retire yet."

He nodded. "Still hard to watch you do it."

"Why? I wouldn't want to stay home. If I had a disabled child or something like that, I think I'd feel differently, but being a doctor is what I've wanted since before we ever met."

"I know. It just doesn't feel right, if that makes any sense at all."

"Not particularly," she said with a grin. "Honestly, I want to work. I don't cook, and I hate to clean. If you want to make me feel like you take care of me, bring someone in to clean once or twice a week. Have them do laundry and the whole nine yards."

He nodded. "We can do that easily."

"You don't mind?"

Nate shook his head. "No, I don't mind at all. How would you feel about going to your work for a bit in the morning, and then looking at some more homes that need to be restored?"

"You're excited to get to the next one, aren't you?"

He nodded. "I'm only still here because I wanted a nice home to bring my wife to when Dr. Lachele found someone for me."

"I'm glad she found me for you," Shelby said. It was hard to be with him and not tell him how much she had hoped they would get back together. And now that they were back together, her heart was singing. But why had he stopped calling her all those years before?

She wanted to trust him implicitly, but she wasn't sure how. He'd stopped calling, and she'd not heard from or seen him. They'd never even broken up, but they'd definitely drifted apart.

They went through some recipes for the Crock Pot together, and she chose some meals. "Maybe we could do some freezer cooking on the weekends. I'm great at organizing."

He shook his head. "I'm not a fan of the way food tastes after having been frozen for so long. Let's just do the slow cooker stuff."

"All right." She thought for a moment. "Who did you hire to clean before I came?" The house had been immaculate, and if the person he'd hired had done such a good job, then perhaps that's who they should have come in weekly.

"A service. One of the neighbors works for them. I could offer her two days a week without going through the company, and we could save a little, and maybe she could quit. She told me she only works a couple days a week anyway." He tilted his head to one side. "Maybe she could do a couple of meals for us as well. Like we leave out a recipe for the days she works, and we have her just make them."

"Great idea! Could we have groceries delivered while she's here so she can put them away?" she asked. "I hate putting groceries away!"

"I do too. Let's see what we can work out with her. I know where she lives, and we can pop over and bother her."

"I hope she likes the idea. It would be nice not to have to worry about that kind of thing and have it magically happen while we're working."

He grinned. "You know, you are the complete opposite of my mom. She's all about being home and taking care of her home. You just want someone else to do it so you can work!"

She nodded. "I'm definitely the opposite of your mom in that."

"I guess it takes every type of person for the world to go round."

"Sure does!"

MONDAY WAS BUSY FOR Nate and Shelby, but it was a good busy. Their neighbor, Tricia, was outside watering her lawn when they walked outside to go to her office. Instead, they walked over and talked to her briefly, explaining what they needed.

Tricia's face lit up at the offer. "I love that idea. I work two days a week for the cleaning service just for extra money. You're offering me more than they pay me, but you're also paying less than you would through them. I think it's a great idea."

"Do you cook?" Shelby asked. "We'd love it if you'd cook and leave it in the oven on the days you're there. We'll even set recipes out until you get used to the type of things we enjoy."

"I love to cook!"

"Yay! I'd rather cut my own nose off than even think about cooking."

Tricia laughed. "What do you do?"

"I'm a doctor. Just finished my fellowships, and I opened a practice here."

"And you two just got married?" Tricia asked.

Nate nodded. "Childhood sweethearts. We were supposed to go to college together but my dad was sick, so I stayed here instead."

"And now you're back together. The romance lover inside me is cheering for you both. That's wonderful!"

"I never dreamed it would take us so long to be together again, but I always hoped it would happen," Shelby said, looking at Nate.

"How long have you two been married?" Tricia asked.

"Two days," Nate said, grinning at her reaction. "I'm too busy at this time of year to take a honeymoon, but I'm hoping we can take one in a few months."

"And I'm too busy getting my practice off the ground," Shelby said. "There'll be lots of time for vacations in the next sixty years."

Nate glanced at her. "Is that how long we'll be married?" he asked.

"That all depends on your cholesterol, doesn't it?"

He groaned, looking at Tricia. "She's going to steal my blood in a few minutes, and she needs to remind me to torment me. Let us know when you can start."

"I work Wednesday and Friday this week. I could do Tuesday and Thursday and give notice."

"Perfect! Or you can keep working for them, if you want to get further ahead financially," Nate said.

"Sounds like you're a saver."

"I am. My house is just a flip for me. It's ready to sell now. All the money I make goes into the next bigger house, and then I do that one."

"Oh, that's wonderful. My husband has always wanted to do that."

"You should have him talk to me." He raised his hand in a wave. "But for now, Shelby's going to play vampire."

Tricia laughed. "I hope she's good!"

"She's wonderful," Nate said, knowing his Shelby would never hurt him.

Chapter Five

At Shelby's office, Nate sat with Rachel behind the counter, and showed her the best program for payroll and how he thought she should do it. He also showed her the best program for keeping books, and explained step-by-step what he felt she should do to keep on top of the finances.

While he was doing that, Shelby spent a few minutes in her office looking at test results. She found Aunt Lydia's and nodded, seeing they were exactly what she'd expected. She'd put Aunt Lydia on a diet that would help her control her diabetes, and she felt like the older woman would feel a ton better. Maybe she could even get off her insulin shots.

After a few minutes of looking at all the results, she went into the reception area to get Nate's blood.

She rolled up his sleeve and took the blood while he kept explaining about the program he'd had Rachel purchase, showing her how to put that purchase into the program.

Before eleven, they were both done, and they left the office to meet their real estate agent for lunch.

They went to the Olive Garden that was a short distance from her office and met with a married couple, who both worked for the same agency. "I know you guys will need to look through my house to come up with what you think we should ask for it, and I'll base what kind of home we want to buy on that amount," Nate said. "I want something bigger and nicer this time. Well, it can be bigger and crappier, but in a good neighborhood, because I'll make it nicer."

Shelia, the wife, looked at Shelby. "You don't have any opinions about it?"

Shelby shrugged. "I trust Nate. He's the one flipping houses. I can live just about anywhere. I just moved from a house I shared with three other women in a rundown neighborhood near the teaching hospital where we all worked. I can survive anywhere."

Shelia nodded, making a quick note on the pad in front of her. "There's a house from the old part of town that was absolutely the most beautiful house in town, but it's fallen into disrepair. Now the family is selling it because the mother who has lived there for her entire married life is going into a nursing home. They want the house to pay for as much of their mother's care as possible."

Nate nodded. "Sounds like a good place to start. What are they asking?"

"Six-seventy-five, which I know is a lot, but I think you'll get close to that for the house you're in, and then small payments. And this house will go for millions once it's fixed up."

He nodded, obviously thinking seriously about it. Shelby was surprised he was willing to spend that much, or that he even was able to spend so much, but she knew he was wise with his finances. He always had been. "Let's look at it."

"Good!" Shelia said. "I think it's the perfect flip house for someone with your skills."

"Let's drive by ours first," Nate said. "If you don't think I can get at least six for it, then I don't think I'll be willing to sink that kind of money into it."

"Of course," Shelia said. Her husband appeared to be just along for the ride.

Shelia and Rick followed Nate and Shelby to the house they lived in. While he drove, Nate explained, "Shelia sold me this house and the last six I've flipped. It takes me about two years to make most of them ready for someone else. I work through the winters, and even have to bring the crew in at times, but I keep buying more expensive homes and selling them. It's working for me."

"I had no idea that sort of thing was so lucrative!"

"I've been doing this since we were about twenty," he said. "I started with a house that was just over fifty thousand, and sold it for eighty-five. After that, it just made sense to keep doing it. I seriously love the work, and with my sister's help, I've always turned a nice profit."

He pulled into the driveway, and the other couple pulled in behind them. "They're going to check out the whole house, but they aren't going to be bothered if something is a little messy, so don't worry as you see them going into our bedroom and kitchen."

"I've never owned a house to sell it. I'm glad to hear they're thorough."

When they went inside, the older couple went from room to room, making notes, and finally came back down. "You'll get six hundred for this easy. What did you pay? I'm thinking it was less than three hundred."

Nate nodded. "And I put about two hundred into it and lived here for two years. Not too shabby."

"Not at all," Shelia said. "Can I list it immediately?"

He nodded. "Sounds good to me. Would be nice if we were in a new place by winter."

"The home I'm going to show you first is the one I think you'll want. It's one of the older homes, in an older ritzy neighborhood, and it needs a ton of work. There's a pool, but it's overgrown and gross."

"Let's go see it then!" Nate said.

When they got into the car, Shelby asked him, "We want a house with a gross pool?"

"It won't be gross when I'm finished with it," he said. "The whole point in doing this is to make money off them, and the nicer the house to start with, the more it will go for. Being in one of the older neighborhoods will give it more value. You'll see."

They followed the other couple to the house they were thinking about, and Nate looked at it from the outside with a huge smile. "This will go for two million when I'm done with it."

"You think?" she asked. The windows were dirty and everything about it was rundown.

"I bet it has good bones. Houses that were built in this time period always have good bones."

They got out and walked up to the front door, and Shelia unlocked it with the key in the lockbox. As they walked through the house, she explained that the matron of the family, who was in the nursing home had advanced Alzheimer's. "No one was visiting much because she'd been angry, so they didn't realize how bad it was getting or how rundown the house had become. When her doctor called her oldest son and told him it was time for her to go to a nursing home, he was really upset with himself with how bad the house looked." She shook her head. "But she's in one of those nursing homes with a sixties restaurant that does sock hops every other week. The residents love it there, and they think they still live in the sixties, so it's good for all of them."

"I'm glad she ended up in a good place," Shelby said. "I have worked with Alzheimer's patients, and they are always so confused. That type of home is the best place for them in my opinion."

"What do you do?" Shelia asked.

"I'm a doctor."

"Oh, well then you'd know!" As they walked through the house, there was a lot of work that needed to be done. Wallpaper was coming off the walls, and paneling was hanging. The appliances in the kitchen looked like they were at least forty years old. So much work needed to be done, and Shelby would have been overwhelmed by it all.

"I will want a termite inspection," Nate finally said. "Everything else I can deal with, but termites would be too much. I'll offer six-fifty."

Shelia smiled, nodding. "I have the forms here if you want to make your offer."

Nate started to fill out the form, but then hesitated and looked at Shelby. "Are you okay if we do this?"

She shrugged. "I'll have a roof over my head and you by my side. I'll be fine." She'd almost said a roof over my head and you in my bed, but she'd thought better of it. She'd wait another month or two before rhyming silly things.

He finished the form and handed it to Shelia. "I don't need to see anything else. This house is what I've been dreaming about fixing up my whole life."

Shelia grinned. "Think you'll stay here?"

"I doubt it. There are too many houses to fix up to stick with one."

As they drove home, Shelby thought about what he'd said. "Are we going to keep buying houses and selling them through our whole marriage?" She liked the idea of the kids having some stability.

He frowned. "We could always do this one, and then buy a house for us to keep, and I could keep doing flip houses on my own time. We just wouldn't have to live in them."

She nodded. "I think that would be better. The children that I'm determined to have will need the stability."

"How many kids do you want?" he asked.

"Oh, two or three. I don't need to repopulate the earth on my own, but I would love to have a couple."

"Two or three sounds good," he said. "I was worried you wanted ten kids or something, and I was trying to figure out who would raise them with us both working."

"I'm not terribly worried about that," she said. "We'll get a good nanny, and we'll be with them as much as we can."

He nodded, not even liking the idea of a nanny. "I bet Mom would watch them while we worked."

"That would work when they're little," Shelby agreed. "When they're older, it would just be a couple of hours after school they'd need care. We'd be home as much as they were."

"All right. I think that'll work." Nate wasn't sure how to say it, but as much as he cared for her and wanted her to be happy with her job, he didn't like the idea of their kids being raised by nannies. He was sure he was just old-fashioned, but he was happier this way.

"I could always move to a bigger office and have a nursery right there if a nanny or your mom won't work. That way, I could be with them when they needed to be fed and see them in the office. Hiring someone to care for them during office hours sounds smart to me."

"We'll think on it," he said. "I'm sure we're going to be happy with whatever we decide."

They spent the rest of the day getting her belongings from her mother's house. There were more clothes and other things she'd gathered over the years. It didn't take terribly long, but every time they went to her mother's house, she ended up talking to her mother for a while.

"Are you happy?" Mom asked.

Shelby nodded. "I'm cautiously happy. I love Nate, but I didn't like the way he broke things off with me by just not calling. I have to be able to trust him again before I can be completely happy."

"That makes sense," Mom said. "I was thrilled to see that it was him you were marrying, and not a stranger."

"I was too, to be honest with you. I'm not sure how I'd be adjusting if he'd been an actual stranger."

"He wouldn't have been a stranger for long," Mom said.

"That's true, but it's better this way. We'll work through all our stuff and be happy together. I've never been able to picture myself married to anyone but Nate anyway."

"You two always did seem to be right for each other. As against young marriages as I am, I think I would have approved of you two marrying after college like you talked about."

"I think it might be better this way," Shelby said. "We've both been on our own, and we know more about what we want now."

Mom nodded.

Nate came out of her old bedroom with one last box. "This is it," he said. "Let's get this last box home and figure out something for supper."

"DoorDash again?" Shelby asked.

He nodded. "I'm not up to cooking after moving you. And I'm sure you're tired from all the talking you've been doing," he said.

Shelby grinned. "Definitely. I may have to prescribe some throat lozenges for myself."

He laughed. "Come on. Let's finish this up."

Shelby hugged her mom. "See you in a few days, I'm sure."

"I'll be here," Mom said. "I'm glad you're home."

"I think I am too," Shelby said with a smile. "I never thought I'd want to move back to Scranton, but I'm happy."

Shelby stood and followed Nate out the door, glad to be going home with him and not staying with her mother. Her mother still made her feel like a child, though she knew Mom didn't mean to. Being with Nate made her feel like she was a teenager and a grown woman all at once. He brought back so many memories.

On the drive back to their house, she rested her head on the headrest, watching him drive. "Did you have to ride with Dr. Lachele?" she asked.

"No, but she ran over Mom's azalea bushes."

"She ran over our mailbox, and almost killed me like ten times. Someone needs to take her license away from her."

He chuckled. "She paid for the bushes."

"And for the mailbox. I think that's how she gets away with it all. Even though she's destroying things, she fixes them without getting the police involved."

"That is probably true. Sorry you had to ride with her."

"That's okay. She took me out for the best steak I've ever eaten to make up for it."

"Where?" he asked.

"Ruth's Chris Steakhouse. It's part of the casino."

"Ah," he said. "We'll have to go there one of these days. I'm always in the mood for a good steak."

When he pulled into their driveway, he had his door half open when she stopped him by putting her hand on his arm. "I'm really glad we're married. Thanks for moving me while I spent all day talking to my mom."

He grinned. "I know she's really missed you. Maybe even more than I have."

She put her arms around him and kissed him. "It feels like we've been apart for so long, and like we've never been away from each other all at once. Isn't that crazy?" she asked.

He nodded. "It is crazy, but it's exactly how I feel. I'm so glad you're back in Scranton and here with me."

They stayed in the truck in their embrace for a few minutes, and then he whispered, "Are you hungry?"

Nothing made her move as quickly as the thought of food did.

Chapter Six

Shelby wished she'd taken a full week off after the wedding, and she said as much to Nate as they were getting ready for work the following day. "We should have taken a week or two," she said. She was still exhausted from her fellowships, and here she was working constantly. A vacation felt like a necessity at the moment.

He nodded. "I just can't at this time of year. We'll take a week this winter."

"Sounds good. We should go somewhere hot to get away from the cold for a change." She'd always dreamed about living somewhere that didn't have a ton of snow every year.

"I'd like that. I'll start looking into warm weather vacations this evening. Tricia starts here today, so I'm going to head over there to give her the keys before I leave this morning."

She nodded, grabbing a bowl and filling it with cereal and milk. "I'm glad that'll be taken care of. It should make life a little easier." She had an appointment with Aunt Lydia that day, and she wasn't looking forward to having to come down on her about her diet. And she had a feeling everything she said would get back to her mother.

"Do you have a full day of work today?" he asked.

She nodded. "I do. Back-to-back appointments, which is good and bad. I like that I'm helping people, and the money will be nice, but I kind of want to take a nap between patients."

He chuckled. "Are you going to change your name?" he asked.

"I think I want to keep my name to use professionally, but I'll use your name for real life, if that makes sense."

He nodded. "You've worked hard to get where you are. Your name is part of it."

"It is." She looked at him. "Do you mind?"

He shook his head. "Not at all. I don't think women should have to change their name if they don't want to anyway."

After breakfast, they both headed out the door, her to her office and him to his own. "My car is still at Mom's," she said, frowning. "Can you give me a lift to work? I can get Rachel to take me to get my car at lunchtime."

He nodded. "I can. Let me run over and talk to Tricia, and then I'll be right back."

Instead of waiting, she walked over with him. Tricia was dressed and ready to go, so she was happy to see them. "We just put our house on the market yesterday," Shelby told Tricia. "There may be people coming to see the house."

Tricia nodded. "I'll bake some cookies so it'll smell more welcoming."

"Just make sure you leave a few for us," Nate said with a grin.

Tricia laughed. "I'm making them in your house, which makes them yours."

"I like the way you think," he said, handing her a key.

"Good, then we'll get along great. Where will you move?"

"Oh, we found a house in the old part of town. I'm really excited to start working on it."

Tricia smiled. "Sounds like you're going to have fun with it then. I'll make supper and leave it in a warm oven for you."

As they walked back to the car, Shelby said, "I hope she'll continue to clean for us once we move. She's so sweet, and I feel like we can really trust her."

He drove her the short distance to work, and before she left his truck, she slid across the seat for one last kiss before their jobs separated them for the first time after they were married.

"Have a good day," she said softly.

"I'll see you this evening."

"Wait!" she said.

"What?"

"Tricia has a key to our house, and I don't yet."

He laughed. "Maybe you'll need to get in, huh?"

"I would certainly like to."

He took an extra key from his keychain and handed it to her. "There. Should help."

"See ya!" she said, her mouth aching to say she loved him, but she wasn't ready for that yet. How did she tell a man she loved him when they'd been parted for so long? It would put her heart in danger, and she couldn't risk that.

She walked into the building from the back, walking through to find Rachel at her desk and a few patients already checking in for their appointments. "We're a little early, but let's get started," Shelby told her sister. "I think it would be good to get ahead for a change. I hate waiting for doctors."

"I'm sure they do too," Rachel said.

Shelby had patients all day, some there with minor complaints, and some there with serious concerns. It was a good mix, and she was glad once again that she'd chosen to go into family practice. She had a chance to treat patients with all different complaints this way.

Her last patient of the day was a woman who was about to burst with twins. "Are you sure you want to change doctors this far into your pregnancy?" Shelby asked.

"Positive," the woman said. "The doctor I was seeing told me that I was bigger than a house, and it was time to stop indulging myself with this pregnancy. I've lost ten pounds since I got pregnant!"

"That's weird," Shelby said, shaking her head. "I don't know why they'd say that. As far as I can see, you're just the size you should be." Shelby knew the other woman had started out heavy, but she didn't think doctors should be complaining about weight gain when there'd been loss. It made no sense. Pregnant women needed to be handled carefully anyway.

"You shouldn't have more than another few weeks to go. You have my after hours number in case you go into labor in the middle of the night, right?"

The patient nodded. "All my other babies came in the middle of the night. I see no reason these two will do things any differently."

"How many children do you have now?" Shelby asked.

"Four, so these two are five and six. And then I'm getting my tubal."

"Done, are you?"

"Exhausted," the patient replied. "Six children under the age of ten should be enough for everyone."

Shelby nodded. "I agree. I don't know how you do it."

"At the moment?" the patient said, "I'm held together by stress and static cling."

Shelby laughed. "Well, hopefully once these two are born, you'll feel like yourself again. Is there anything I can do to make your life easier?"

"Induce tomorrow?"

"They need another two weeks if they can get it. You'll thank yourself when you're holding your healthy babies."

"I know. I just wish it could be all over. I'm not looking forward to giving birth again."

Shelby helped her patient off the exam table. "I'll see you next week."

"I'll be here."

As the woman waddled out to the front and left, Shelby went to Rachel. "What does my schedule look like tomorrow."

Rachel shook her head. "I just had someone call sick, and you can't see them til next week."

"What were the symptoms?" Shelby asked.

"Coughing, sneezing, cold symptoms."

"Have they taken a Covid test?" Shelby asked.

"I don't know."

"If you would, call them and find out. There are certain things I'd want to prescribe depending on their medical history. If they've taken the test and it's negative, book them during my lunch tomorrow."

Rachel nodded, flipping to another page in the book in front of her and making the call. When she finished, she looked at Shelby. "She took a home test, and it was negative. She'll be here at noon."

"Sounds good. Just grab me extra of whatever you get for lunch, and take it out of petty cash," Shelby said. She knew she and her sister had very similar tastes when it came to food. "I think tacos are in order..."

Rachel laughed. "Tacos are always in order!"

When Shelby got home, Nate's truck wasn't in the driveway yet. She used her key and unlocked the door, walking in to find Tricia still there. "I thought you'd be long gone!"

Tricia shrugged. "I was doing laundry and kind of lost myself. I did tablecloths and all kitchen towels."

Shelby smiled. "You are the best!"

"I've got one last load in the dryer. Do you mind if I stay and finish it?"

"Do I mind if you do my laundry? No!"

Tricia laughed. "How long have you known Nate?"

"We were high school sweethearts," she said. "We meant to go to the same college, but his dad got sick, and he was needed. So I moved away, and he stayed here, and we kind of drifted apart."

Tricia frowned. "That's sad. I'm glad you're back together now."

"I am too. I always saw myself with Nate."

While Tricia folded the last load of laundry, she said, "A real estate agent brought someone through today, but they didn't mind me being here. I asked."

"Did they seem to like it?" Shelby asked. She was in love with the house and almost wished they didn't need to sell it. But she understood the concept of flipping houses, and it made sense."

Tricia nodded. "They did. The couple has three kids, and they like the idea of everyone getting their own room. The wife wanted to put down an offer right away, but the husband insisted they look at the rest of the houses on their list."

"I hope they make an offer. I don't know how long I can keep Nate from working on the next house, and he wants the money from this one to buy it."

"That makes sense. Is there a lot of work to be done on the new one?"

Shelby shrugged. "Kind of looks like a heap of trash to me, but Nate's whole face lit up. He said it was perfect, and it had good bones. Whatever that means."

"We really need to get our husbands together. Jeff would love Nate."

"He took pictures of this place before he fixed it up. I have no idea where said pictures live, but maybe we could have you guys over on Saturday for supper, and Nate could show off his skills."

"He'd have a very willing audience in Jeff."

"Let's plan on that then. Nate will make something fantastic for dinner. I would cook, but I'm kind of limited to ramen and grilled cheese sandwiches. Nate has all the cooking skills."

Tricia smiled. "Let me know what he's making, and I'll make something to go with it."

"I can do that."

Finishing folding the last towel, Tricia said, "I should head home. Jeff will be there soon, and he likes me to be home when he gets there."

"Sounds good. I had no idea when Nate will be here. I have to guess he's working late."

"It is the busy season for construction."

"I know. Doesn't mean I don't wish he was here," Shelby said with a smile. "I'm a newlywed, and I think it's my job to miss him or something."

Tricia laughed. "We've been married for three years. I still miss him."

"I guess I'm not insane then."

"Not at all. Okay, I'm done. I'm going to put your laundry away and head home. Supper is in the oven. Just keep it on warm, and you'll be happy with it."

After Tricia was gone, Shelby peeked in the oven. Whatever it was, smelled delicious. When she saw it was enchiladas, she wanted to jump up and down with joy. Mexican food made the whole world go round, and she didn't care who argued with her. They were wrong.

When she heard the front door open, Shelby rushed into the living room to greet Nate. She threw her arms around him and kissed him. "It feels like today took forever."

He chuckled. "I missed you too." His arms were around her, but she could see the weariness on his face.

"Tough day?" she asked, taking his hand and pulling him toward the couch.

"Not tough, just long. We were knocking out walls and putting up new sheetrock today. Always feels like a forever long day."

"I'll serve supper. Tricia has it keeping warm in the oven for us."

"Let me get a quick shower. I'm covered in grime. I'll be ready to eat in ten minutes."

"Hurry, or I'll eat all the food," she warned him.

"As sad as that statement is, I completely believe you. The enchiladas smell delicious."

"I think she did ground beef with sour cream sauce, which is my absolute favorite."

"I'll hurry."

By the time he was back downstairs, the table was set, and she had taken the enchiladas from the oven. She served them both three of the enchiladas, and added some of the rice and beans Tricia had made as sides.

"Oh, your cholesterol is fine," she said. "Got the results back this morning."

"So I can eat all the cheese and red meat I want?"

She sighed. "Everything in moderation."

"I'd like to see you eat that in moderation," he said. "I know how much you love those enchiladas. Your mom used to make them."

"She was stationed in Texas during the Gulf War, and she worked in a couple of different restaurants there. I wouldn't trade her ability to cook good Tex-Mex for anything."

He laughed, taking her hand and praying over their meal. As soon as they'd said amen, she cut off a bite and ate it. "Oh, this is wonderful! Did you get the recipe from my mom?"

"Sure did. I thought it might make you feel welcomed."

"It did. No doubt about that." She took another large bite, this time scooping some of the beans on her fork as well. "Now, if we just had queso..."

He laughed. "I'm sure we'll have queso soon."

"I invited Tricia and Jeff to supper on Saturday night. If you don't want to cook, we'll order something in."

"Sounds good."

"Tricia said he'll want to see the before and after pics of the house."

"I have them in a photo album upstairs. I'll make sure I show them. I probably should have taken the time to make friends with Jeff before. Sounds like we have a lot in common."

"I agree," Shelby said. "Tricia said he would go nuts over all the work you've done here. You should invite him to help with the next house. I can't call it a new house, because it's definitely not new, but it's going to be beautiful."

"Yeah, I'd be happy to let him help if he really wants to." Nate finished eating and pushed his plate away. "I think we'll have enough for tomorrow night too."

"I don't know. I haven't had my bedtime snack yet," Shelby said, eyeing the enchiladas and wondering if she could eat just one more. They sure sounded good.

Chapter Seven

By Friday afternoon, Shelby was dragging. It had been a busy week, and all she wanted to do was spend the weekend with Nate.

He was home before she was, which was a good sign, and she hurried inside. He was sitting on the couch, watching more cooking videos. "I didn't plan anything for supper," he said, having no idea what they would do.

"We can go out or order something in," she said. She had no desire to go out, but if he wanted to, she would.

"I'm too tired to eat out," he said. "Let's order in."

"Exactly my thoughts," she said. "I'd have gone with you if you wanted to go out, but I wouldn't have liked it one little bit."

"You should have told me that. You're allowed to make decisions like that too, you know."

"I know." She tucked her feet under her as she sat down beside him. She was still wearing her scrubs and really just wanted to take a three-hour bath and lose herself in a romance novel.

He looked at her, and he could see the fatigue on her face. "You should go get in the bathtub and read for a while. You look exhausted."

"Would you mind? And you can order for me. It's not like you don't know what I like to eat."

He smiled. "I used to have your favorite thing at every restaurant memorized."

"I remember. You were the best."

"I was? I'm not now?"

She smiled, brushing his lips with hers. "I have to get to know you all over again before I can answer that. In the next house, you need to make a bathtub big enough for two."

As she wandered away from him, he grinned. It would take a while, but he was sure he could get her to fall in love with him again. He didn't need to worry about it for him. He was still in love with her after all those years. Just seeing her again told him all he needed to know.

Shelby stripped in the bathroom and climbed into the tub. It had a jacuzzi jet, and she was more than happy to turn it on as she picked up her book. This wasn't a bath for getting clean. No, she was just going to soak the day away.

Too quickly after she'd gotten in, Nate called her on her book...er...phone. "Yes?"

"Food will be here in a minute. You may want to get dressed and come down."

"On my way." She wished she could just eat in the bathtub, and for a moment, she thought about asking Nate to bring her food up to the bathroom, but then she decided to be an adult and go all the way downstairs. Eating with Nate was something she looked forward to.

She got downstairs as he was pulling their food out of bags and putting it on the table. "Italian?" she asked, surprised. It wasn't that she didn't like Italian, but he was always catering to her and getting her tacos.

He nodded. "Yeah, the local Italian place does this pizza taco thing. They roll up taco meat in a pizza crust, and then serve it with lettuce, tomato, and sour cream. I thought you might like to try it."

"Oh, yeah!" she said. "Anytime someone can combine a pizza with a taco, I know they're doing something right."

"I also got cheese-stuffed breadsticks. We'll be in carb overload, but we'll be happy."

After their prayer, she took a bite of one of the rolls, and smiled. "I think there are beans in there too. I can taste them. You're right. This is delicious."

"I got a chicken one if you want to trade."

She nodded. "Absolutely." She gave him half of her rolls and took half of his. Then she bit down into one of the breadsticks and sighed contentedly. "Good choice of meals."

"It's a new thing they're doing, but I think it'll stick around. It's just so good!"

"What are you planning for supper for Tricia and Jeff tomorrow night?" she asked.

He shrugged. "I figured I'd do a taco bar. Serve queso, beans, cheese, and meat along with chips, tortillas and shells, and everyone can assemble their own meal."

"Like we did for the wedding," she said with a smile.

"Exactly. And I'm going to try my hand at sopapillas. I do love sopapillas."

"Oh, I'll look forward to those. We have butter and cinnamon and honey?"

"I have all the essentials. I made Tricia a grocery list and she hit the store yesterday while she was here. Are you happy with the work she's doing?" he asked.

"Ecstatic! Next time let me know when you're making a grocery list though. I want more variety in my morning cereal."

"We could make breakfast casseroles if you'd rather. I can Crock Pot them the night before, or we can assemble it all and leave it in the fridge overnight. Either way it'll be delicious."

"That sounds good," she said, pursing her lips. "Yeah, let's start doing that. How long do they have to cook if we just assemble then?"

"About thirty minutes," he said. "I could come down and get it started while you shower in the mornings."

She nodded. "Great idea. Let's start that this week. I feel like my cereal is wearing off by ten, and then I need to eat early, and there's no time between patients. Actually eating eggs and bacon would thrill me."

"Easy enough. I may even teach you to make some of them."

"Do you have to?" she asked, grinning at him.

"I think you need to be able to cook simple things. Everyone should be able to."

"I guess you're right. I won't like it, but I'll do it."

After supper, she threw away their paper products the food had come in and joined him in the living room. "I think we need to shut our minds off and vegetate in front of the television tonight."

"I can agree with that. What do you want to watch?"

She shrugged. "I have no idea of any shows from the past twelve years or so. Just something relatively new would work for me."

He nodded, flipping the television to Amazon Prime and choosing *Big Bang Theory*. He had a hunch she would love it.

They were six episodes in before she yawned. "I think I need to sleep. I like this show though. But Sheldon needs an official diagnosis. The man isn't crazy, but he is autistic."

They went up to bed together, and she realized he was dragging as much as she was. She was exhausted, but he was just as bad.

Instead of putting on one of her pretty little night things she'd been wearing for him, she put on an old beat-up pair of Snoopy pajamas and climbed into bed. He noticed and grinned. "Does this mean you're too tired for hanky panky?"

"Well, you know that I like hanky and panky, but right now, I'm just not sure I could stay awake through it. I'll make it up to you tomorrow."

He nodded, climbing into bed beside her and pulling her close. Even if they weren't going to make love, he was going to hold her during the night. There was no point in being married if they couldn't touch.

As soon as Shelby woke the following morning, she glanced at the clock and saw that it was after ten. She couldn't remember the last time she'd slept so late. Even on Saturdays, it had been her habit to pore over medical books to learn all she could.

Nate was already awake, and he'd shut the door so he wouldn't wake her.

She went downstairs, still in her Snoopy pajamas to see what he was up to. She found him in the kitchen, removing a breakfast casserole from the oven. "That smells delicious," she said.

He nodded. "Yeah, this is one I just found the recipe for. I don't know if you've ever enjoyed the Southern treat of eggs with biscuits and sausage gravy, but this recipe has it all. I think we're going to love it."

"I have had that. It's served a lot in hotels, and when I've been to medical conferences, I made the most out of the hotels' free breakfasts."

"Well, then you should like this." He poured them each a glass of orange juice and served two large pieces of casserole for them.

When she took her first bite, she moaned softly. "This is delicious. Did it take a long time to make?"

He shook his head. "Only about twenty minutes of prep time."

"That's not bad at all. Especially with as good as it is." As they ate they talked about their plans for the day.

"I'll want to start cooking around six. You said they'd be here around seven, right?"

She nodded emphatically. "Yup. What else do you have planned?"

"Well, you can stay, or you can come with me, but our offer was accepted on the new house, and I've been given permission to start working. They said whatever I wanted to do to make it livable was fine. We're closing next Saturday anyway."

"You've gotten an offer on this place?" she asked.

He nodded. "Better than I expected as well. We're selling this place for six-fifty, and buying that one for the same. It'll be a wash until I start pouring money into repairs and renovation."

"You want to go over and start working on it today?" she asked.

He nodded. "I want to get that bathroom fixed before we move in. We need one bathroom that we're comfortable using."

She nodded. "All right. Do you want me to come or stay?"

He shrugged. "Either way. If you'd rather stay here and relax, that's fine, but if you want to come with me, I'd enjoy your company."

"I'll come with you," she said. "I want to see how you do this stuff."

"I don't expect you to do any of the actual work," he said. "It would be fun to get your opinions on all the fixtures and the color you think the bathroom should be. I want this place to just scream luxury when I'm done."

"Sounds good to me," she said. "Let me change into something that's presentable enough to be out of the house in."

"Nothing nice," he warned. "I'll wear some old jean shorts and a t-shirt for this."

"Then I'll wear shorts and a t-shirt too. I don't have a lot of clothes that I would worry about ruining. A couple of business suits for the conventions I've done."

"Makes sense," he said.

A short while later, they were out of the house and on their way to the new place. He went straight up to the master bath, with her following closely behind. "I'm going to replace this tub entirely," he said. "That corner is going to be a separate shower."

He went to the bathroom counter. "This will be done with double sinks. And I'm going to put a floor to ceiling mirror over here, so you can check your appearance in the mirror before going out."

"You've already got all those ideas after looking at it once?" she asked, surprised.

He nodded. "I've done this before, remember. I came through here, looking for what I could do to update the house and do it well. I'll have a pool guy come in and deal with the pool as soon as we close." He walked into the attached bedroom. "I think we should have two full walk-in closets here. Each one with a bench, so it can be used as a dressing room."

"I'm really impressed. I can see your visions, and I like them. The bedroom itself seems all right, but that peeling wallpaper has got to go."

He nodded. "I'll steam it off, and then paint it."

"And that mirror on the ceiling definitely needs to be history."

"That I will not argue with. I've never understood why they were so popular in the seventies."

He led her out onto the balcony that was off the bedroom. "I think I want a hot tub out here. It would modernize the house some, but it would also be nice after a busy day."

"It would! A sauna might be nice too, but I have no idea where you'd put it."

"I'll think about it," he said. "For now, I'm going to shut off the water and start pulling this tub out."

"Do you need my help?" she asked.

"No, I'd rather you weren't in there while I did it."

"All right," she said. "I may sit on the porch, soak up the sun, and read for a while, if you don't mind."

"Not at all. You bring a book?"

She held up her phone. "This is my book. I can't understand why people think I should use it as a phone."

He laughed. "Go sit."

There was a bench on the balcony that looked as though it had been built in. She made good use of it, reading and looking out over the town. This house really did have a lot of potential, especially after she'd better seen Nate's visions for it.

They stayed there until four before heading home. "I got more accomplished than I thought I would," he told her. "I think I would be comfortable with us moving in a month from now."

"When does the other house close?" she asked.

"It'll be about a month, so we'll want to be able to move in then. I may bring my crew in to help with the kitchen, so it'll be up and running, but I'll do most of the work with my own two hands."

"I'm really impressed with what you've learned to do. I know you didn't like working for your dad when we were younger, but you seem to really enjoy this type of work now."

He nodded. "When I was a teenager, I was trying not to go into the family business. I didn't want to work with my hands. As an adult, I've realized that this is what I was meant to do. I still love the business aspect of things, and I save a lot of money by doing my own books and managing my own finances, but getting my hands dirty and tearing a room apart to recreate it? That's a true joy for me."

"I think that's great," she said. "Your dad would be really proud if he could see you today."

He nodded. "I had tripled his business within three years of taking it over, and he was always telling me what a good job I was doing. I'm glad I pleased him, but a little part of me still wants to sit behind a desk."

She nodded. "I understand. I did what I dreamed I would do, and I still sometimes wonder if I'm going to be able to keep up. I wonder if I actually am good enough to be a doctor."

"There's no doubt about that in my mind," he said. "You're awfully special just the way you are."

Chapter Eight

As they got their taco bar ready that night, Shelby was put on grated cheese duty. "I never thought about the everyday tasks of being married to you," she said. "I guess I thought it would all be jumping into bed together."

Nate grinned at her. "I think we have plenty of that going for us."

"I know we do. But the hard work starts after the wedding. I guess I always thought that as soon as we married, our happily ever after would begin, and there would never be day-to-day monotony again."

"There will always be monotony. It's up to us to make life more exciting, but we must work at that."

"So, what can I do to make grating cheese more exciting?" she asked.

"You should name the block of cheese Charles," he said.

She raised an eyebrow. "Oh?"

"And then you should name each piece of shredded cheese Chip."

"And how does that help me?" She had an awful feeling in the pit of her stomach that this was going to be a terrible corny joke.

"They'll all be Chips off the old block!"

She groaned. "You don't even have to be a dad to tell awful jokes. I don't know what we're going to do when you are a dad, and your jokes deteriorate even more."

He grinned. "That was an awesome joke, and you know it. You just don't have a sense of humor."

"Oh, I have a sense of humor. It just doesn't lend itself to corny jokes."

"That's too bad," he said. "I feel awful for the football team who always practices in the cornfield. They get creamed."

She groaned again. "That one was really bad."

"The corn was worried it was getting sick. Its voice was a little husky."

"No more! I can't take it!"

"The corn farmer was nominated for the Nobel Peace Prize for his dedication to world hominy."

"I don't think I can speak to you anymore," she said. "I may need to bring some ear plugs home from my office so I can stick them in my ears when the occasion warrants."

"You know what happens when you drop your corn on the cob and yell at it?"

"I don't think I can handle any more jokes!"

"It falls on deaf ears."

"Are you done?"

He stood for a moment, thinking about it. "I guess I am."

"I'm so glad!"

He drained the taco meat before adding seasoning. She noticed he didn't use a seasoning packet, but she didn't want to ask what he did use. She was afraid of the answer.

They put each of the toppings into a different bowl, and laid them out on the counter, and she went to get chips from the pantry. They were corn chips, and she hoped it wouldn't open the dam of his *corny* jokes again.

She mentally groaned at her own joke. If this kept up, it was going to be a very long night.

When the doorbell rang, Shelby rushed to go to the door. She was excited to meet Jeff, and she knew she'd have a good time with Tricia. "Welcome!"

Tricia smiled. "Thanks for having us. This is Jeff, and Jeff, this is Shelby."

"Good to meet you," Jeff said, smiling.

"You too! Dinner will be ready in just a minute. Nate is in the kitchen finishing everything up. He's in a mood though, so I hope you don't mind bad jokes."

Tricia laughed. "Bad jokes are always good. I've had contests to see who can make everyone else groan the loudest."

"Don't give Nate any ideas!"

They all went into the kitchen. "We just did a taco bar with flour tortillas, taco shells, and chips. We can each make what we want."

"I approve," Jeff said. "Tacos make the world go round."

Nate put his hand out for Jeff to shake. "You think a bit too much like my wife. I may have to ban you from my home."

"Tacos have all the food groups! You can't get any healthier," Shelby said.

"I can't disagree with that," Jeff said.

"What do you do for a living, Jeff?"

Jeff shrugged. "I sell insurance. Tricia's been telling me about your house-flipping. I would love to be able to do that for a living."

"It's just a side business for me," Nate said, "but I do love it. I'll show you pics of this house before I started after supper."

"I want to see the new house as well. It sounds like that one is going to be a lot of fun."

Shelby grinned. "I'm not so sure about fun, but it will be a lot of work."

"That kind of work is a lot more fun than sitting in an office all day," Jeff said.

"Oh, I definitely agree," Nate said. "It's fun to take a house that's been mistreated and restore it to its former glory. So many houses out there aren't properly taken care of, and then someone like me can turn them into a showplace."

"After pictures, would you mind if we went over to your new house?" Jeff asked. "I want to see what you're starting with."

Nate shook his head. "Not at all. This new house is kind of my dream project. I never thought I'd get my hands on something like this."

"Tricia said you did this house on the weekends while working full time. I want to be able to do that," Jeff said.

"It's not that tough to get into," Nate replied. He finished fixing his taco and moved to the dining room where Tricia and Shelby were already sitting waiting on the men.

When Jeff joined them, he kept asking questions about the house they were buying.

"It's in one of the older parts of town," Nate said, "but the house was once a real showpiece. I need to look at who lived there before, but I'm sure it was some of the most prominent people in Scranton."

"Do you have to do anything to get it ready for move in?"

"So much!" Nate said. "We close on this house in a month, so I need to remodel the bathroom and get the bedroom habitable and look at what needs to be done in the kitchen so we can cook in there. Well, other than clean. There's a lot of cleaning to be done in the entire house."

Tricia looked at Shelby, who was happily munching on her nachos. "I think I may have created a monster."

"I'm sure you did," Shelby said. "He's going to want to spend all his time hanging out with Nate, and they're going to tell each other corny jokes, and we're going to be groaning in unison."

"I guess I'll survive it," Tricia said. "He hates his job so much. If he could find a hobby that would pay at least some of the bills, he'd be a happy camper."

Shelby nodded. "I understand. You know, you don't have to be living in the house you're repairing. You could buy a second house and he could fix it up and sell it by working on the weekends."

"I guess that's true..." Tricia seemed unconvinced.

After supper, they went to the living room and Nate shared all the before pictures of the house. "Do you want to see the whole thing?" Nate asked after Jeff had looked at them all.

"I really do. This place was a mess!"

"It was. But it had good bones, and was on a street with houses that were nicer. So I bought it and got it ready. Now this time when I move to a new house, I'm dragging Shelby along with me, and she'll get to see it all happen..."

Shelby smiled. "I'm actually looking forward to it!"

As the two men went through the house, Shelby quickly did the dishes with Tricia's help. "You shouldn't help!" Shelby complained. "I'm not paying you for tonight, and you're always cleaning my house."

"I should help. My husband and I ate more than our share of food, didn't we?"

Shelby smiled. "All right. But remember, I protested!"

"I'll never forget."

"Do you want to go with the guys to the new house?" Shelby asked as she stuck a plate in the dishwasher.

Tricia nodded. "I'm not as interested as Jeff is, but it'll still be cool to watch it all happen."

"It will. Even if it's not my thing it is Nate's thing, and I love him so I'll support him."

"Makes sense to me."

With the dishes done, they went back into the living room to wait for the men. "Is there anything you need to make your job easier?" Shelby asked. "Are there specific cleaning products you prefer?"

Tricia shook her head. "Nah. I can make do with just about anything."

"Sounds good!" Shelby looked up as the men joined them in the living room.

Jeff looked at Tricia. "I can't believe how excited I am to try this now. I could start with a really cheap fixer-upper, and then gradually move onto bigger houses like Nate has."

"Make sure you have me go with you for the first house or two," Nate said. "Some of them are in horrible disrepair, but they can't be fixed up enough to be decent. They need to be condemned."

"All right. If you don't mind. I know you're busy," Jeff said.

"Aren't we all?" Nate asked. "You ready to go see the new old house?"

Jeff nodded. "How should we do this? All together or separate cars?"

Nate shrugged. "I have dual seats in my truck. We could take it."

"All right. Let's go."

Tricia and Shelby followed along behind their men, getting into the back seat, so the two of them could continue discussing what they wanted to do.

It was a short drive to the new house, and Tricia and Shelby stayed quiet as the men talked nonstop about the business of flipping houses. "There are some things I'm good with, and some I have no clue what to do with," Jeff said.

"Oh, I call in crews for some of it. For instance, I shut off the water, and pulled out the bathtub today, but I'll buy the fixtures and hire someone to come in and do the actual plumbing work. Thankfully, I've got a guy on my crew who's a plumber, and he's always looking for a few extra bucks, so he'll work on it one weekend, and then I'll get in and lay the tile and do the painting. I'll build new cabinets myself, but I won't put the sinks in. I have an electrician on my crew, and he'll do anything electrical. I know how, and I know where to buy everything, but then I have him take care of the rest."

"Makes sense," Jeff said, gasping as they pulled into the driveway of the new house, with large trees on either side, delineating where they should drive. "Oh wow! I had no idea it was a house like this! It looks like something out of a Civil War movie!"

"I know! This is truly my dream job. I've done my before pictures, and I'll show you what I have planned and what I've done so far." Nate turned the key to kill the engine, and then the four of them went inside. In each room, Nate explained exactly what he planned to do.

In the kitchen, he explained that he wanted to update all the appliances, create new, modern-looking cabinets, tear up the linoleum and put down tile, as well as build a large island in the middle. "I figure the island will be where the majority of the prep work is done. I'll put double outlets on each end, which will mean plenty of power for all of the kitchen gadgets I find myself using."

"How long will it take you to do a house this size?" Jeff asked.

Nate shrugged. "At least a year. If I'm dead all winter with my business, I can get it done in twelve months. If we're as busy as we were last winter, it'll be eighteen months or so."

"Wow. And you'll just live here with everything all torn up."

Nate nodded. "I'm making sure the master bath and bedroom are done before we move in, but I want the kitchen functional as well. I have a month, so I'm sure to get it done."

"Could you use another pair of hands that will work for free for the knowledge you impart?"

Nate nodded slowly. "I could. There's a lot to be done."

"And it would help me, because after working on this place with you, I'll be ready to take on my own place." Jeff rubbed his hands together excitedly.

"A small place to start," Tricia said, shaking her head. "We want to wait a couple more years before we start having kids, but I don't want them growing up in a construction zone."

"That makes sense," Shelby said. "We want kids soon, but I don't see me putting them in their own room for a while, so it'll work out fine."

"Yeah, I'm thinking a small two or three bedroom house that we can do while we live there. Something like this would be overwhelming."

"It would be for me too," Shelby agreed, "but Nate has worked his way up to a house like this. It's amazing that he turned the house we're in now to such a beautiful place."

"It is!" Tricia said. "I'm not sure Jeff has the skills he needs to do something anywhere near that scale."

"He will after helping Nate with this house," Shelby said. "Nate not only knows what he's doing, but he's a good teacher."

They moved on to the upstairs and kept listening as Nate explained what he wanted to do. When they got to the master bath, Jeff's eyes widened. "How long did it take you to do all this already?"

"We were here for about five hours," Nate said. "Shelby did a great job of staying out of my way, so it didn't take very long. I'll get a couple of guys from my crew to help me get the tub to the dump on Monday, and I'll get what I need shopped for and delivered by Wednesday night. Then I can have my plumber working with me next weekend."

"I'm really amazed at all you do," Jeff said, shaking his head. "And I want to learn to do every little bit of it."

Nate nodded. "I'll teach you."

Chapter Nine

The next month seemed to pass by so quickly, that it was hard to believe they'd been married for five weeks. Nate and Shelby had packed up the whole house, and were moving that weekend.

Tricia had helped a great deal with the packing, and the other couple was helping move them into the new place. Nate had drafted a bunch of his employees to help as well, so things went smoothly.

As soon as everyone else was gone after a feast of pizzas, Shelby sank into the couch, refusing to empty even one box. "Tricia and Mom and Rachel will all be here tomorrow to help unpack," Shelby said with a yawn. "Tricia and I got sheets on the bed before she and Jeff left, so we can sleep. I don't think we'll be able to eat here until we all get the kitchen unpacked, but that's all right."

"Angela isn't coming?" he asked, surprised. She'd always been closer to Angela than she had to Rachel.

"The twins are teething, and she doesn't feel like she can leave them with anyone. All they're doing is crying."

"Probably best if she's staying home then. Anything you can do?"

"She called and asked for advice, and I told her what any pediatrician would. Rub Orajel on their gums, and give them Tylenol if they're running a fever. She wanted to bring them to me, but I can't treat my family, and I wish they'd all get that through their thick heads."

"Probably not anytime soon." He shook his head. "I'm glad I'm not in a job where I can't help my family. Mom is always needing something done. I had to go over there and fix her fence this week. Her poodle has decided the Great Dane next door needs to be the father of her puppies, and Mom doesn't think much of that idea."

"That would not work out well," Shelby agreed. "I'm glad she has you on speed dial."

"I am too. Usually."

"Are you as tired as I am?" she asked.

He shrugged. "Today wasn't much harder than a regular day of work for me, especially with all the help we had. And tomorrow we'll have help unpacking. I don't think I've ever had a move go more smoothly."

"Well, I'm used to being on my feet all day, but not carrying so many boxes."

"You'll feel better soon. Maybe you should soak in the tub. Or use Biofreeze on your feet and legs."

"And arms and shoulders..." She sighed dramatically. "I hope you get that hot tub put in soon."

"I can do that soon," he said. "But we have jets in our master bath."

"We do?"

He nodded. "I told you I was going to do that."

"But I didn't know you had!" She slowly got to her feet, groaning as she held the small of her back. "Now I know why I've kept so little over the years. A few textbooks have been the extent of heavy things I've had to move."

"I don't know if there are towels up there."

"I'll drip dry if I have to!"

"Maybe I'll join you," he said.

"The bathtub is big enough?" she asked, looking over her shoulder.

"Biggest bathtub ever!" he said. "Or rather the biggest one Home Depot had in stock." He followed her toward the stairs. "We're sharing."

She grinned. "I like that we don't even have to think about these things anymore. Remember all the rules we had for making out back in high school?"

"No touching below the waist. Touching above the waist but over the shirt. I was sure all the rules were going to kill me."

"But they didn't, and now we're all grown up, and the rules are forgotten."

"So if I grabbed you now, I could touch below the shirt?"

She laughed. "The shirt will be history in just a minute."

"You're right," he said. "It's much better this way." Though thinking about the past was not good for him. It made him worry she would blow him off again. There was an entire semester where she'd refused to take his calls. Her roommate had said she was at the library studying every single day. He'd always left a message until he realized she'd never call him back.

She started filling the tub before she undressed. When she turned around, he was right behind her doing the same. "I like being able to look at you now, too," she said. "I got tired of just using my imagination about the muscles I felt beneath your shirt."

Nate smiled. "I think my view is better."

She giggled. "I'm not going to argue about that. I feel like we both won."

She got into the tub first, leaning against the foot of it. The tub was large, square, and had a dozen jets. "Why have I gone my whole life without knowing they made bathtubs like this?"

He shrugged. "You should have moved back here sooner. I'd have made sure you knew that this was the ultimate bathtub we were striving for in life."

Her smile faded. She'd heard that he was dating another woman all the time. It seemed now that much of that had been exaggeration, but still...being without him was difficult.

"I guess I came back at just the right time," she finally said, but for her, their celebratory mood was lost.

"I can't say that I'm disappointed to be taking a bath with the girl I've always thought was the most perfect person in the world. I thought your mom messed up when she named you. You should have been Angela, because you're angelic, and Angela could be Shelby."

"I'm anything but angelic, so you can just put that thought right back where you found it." She shook her head. "Are you and Jeff going to work on the house tomorrow? Or are you going to help unpack?"

"It sounds like you have a whole crew to unpack, so we'll work on the house. I want to get new windows in before winter. I have a feeling these will just let the cold in."

She nodded. "All right. Are we allowed to put dishes in cabinets?" She had no idea how soon he'd be starting work on the kitchen, and she didn't want to do anything to slow him down.

"I won't get to the kitchen for a few months yet. There's too much that needs to be done to get the house ready for winter, and all that needs to come first."

"Then we will stuff those cabinets."

He smiled. "I appreciate you going with the flow about where we live. I know it has to seem like I'm obsessed, but so much needs to be done."

"You're allowed to have hobbies that take you from me at times. If I got a call right now that one of my patients was in labor or in the ER, I'd leave without looking back." She hid a yawn behind her hand. "I haven't contributed anything to the household budget and have instead saved all the money I've made for a downpayment on a new car. Do you need me to contribute, or are you good if I get that new car soon?"

He grinned a lopsided grin. She loved his grins. "Go for it. I've seen what you drive, and I swear, it's held together with paperclips and duct tape."

"Masking tape," she corrected. "Duct tape was too expensive."

He shook his head. "I'm afraid that I believe you."

"You should. Okay, car shopping. I'll go after work on Monday."

"I'll pick you up from work, and we'll go together. I don't want you coming home with anything that remotely resembles that car you've been driving."

She laughed. "I wouldn't have purchased that car if I hadn't needed something inexpensive. Now that I can afford something better, I'll get it. Maybe a small-size SUV or something."

"I'll be with you," he said. "It'll be better that way. I promise."

"All right. I'm never going to turn down spending time with you."

At her words, he frowned, thinking of the time he'd offered to go to her school for a weekend just so they could see each other, and she'd never even returned his call. She'd been odd about using her cell phone for only emergencies unless she was on wifi, so he'd stopped calling her on it. What had happened there?

"Well, that's settled then," he said. He knew they were going to need to talk about what happened all those years ago soon, but tonight was not the night. They were both too tired to think about anything like that, and he didn't think they should talk about it when the conversation wasn't going to go well.

Soon, they were in bed, and they were snuggling together. "I need a massage," she told him.

"You should get one!" he replied.

"You wouldn't mind?"

He shook his head. "Our finances are fine. Maybe next Saturday."

"I could probably do Saturday," she said.

"Good. I think it'll be good for you."

"You know, I've never had a massage? Until Dr. Lachele made me get one. I've checked prices a million times, but it never seemed to be a smart way to use my money."

He yawned. "Won't hurt us. I mean, I don't think you should get them daily but a couple times a month would be fine."

She snuggled closer to him. "You're the best husband ever."

When she woke the following morning, Nate wasn't anywhere to be found, which surprised her. She knew he was planning on working all day while she and the other ladies unpacked.

She went downstairs to find him, but he wasn't there either. Finally, she pulled her cell phone from her pocket and called him. "You okay?"

"About to walk in the door," he said.

She hurried to the front door and opened it wide. He was standing there with two bags from McDonalds. "I figured a McDonald's breakfast would be just what the doctor ordered. Oh, hmm...guess I should have asked the doctor."

"Sounds good to me. I need fuel to make it through the day. What did you get me?"

"A breakfast burrito with bacon and hash browns with orange juice."

"Perfect!" She took one of the bags and carried it to the table to help him as he was balancing two orange juices as well.

While they ate, he told her that he and Jeff would be working on some of the windows on the first floor. "I've got to get as many switched out before the snow hits, and it's already mid-October."

"Yeah but we usually don't get snow til late December or even January," she said.

"I want to get the whole house by then. And I need to get the chimney cleaned. We're going to have some beautiful nights in front of that fireplace this winter."

"Fall could work for a night in front of the fireplace as well," she said.

"This is true. I'll schedule that for this week if I can make it work."

Soon all of their helpers descended on them, and the women made short work of unloading the kitchen boxes. "What next?" Mom asked.

"Master bath," Shelby said quickly. "I took a bath last night, and I had to drip dry because we didn't have anything in there unpacked."

When they got to the master bedroom, Tricia said, "I could work a couple of extra days this week if you want. Most of the house could be unpacked by the end of the week that way."

Shelby thought about it for a moment before nodding. "That would help a ton."

By mid-day, they'd done a few rooms, and Shelby grabbed her phone. "I'm going to order a bunch of different foods from Olive Garden, and then we can all just eat family style."

"Perfect," Mom said, wiping her hands on her jeans. "I cannot wait to see this house when it's done. Nate is a genius."

"He is," Rachel said.

While the others talked, Shelby put in a DoorDash order for Olive Garden before putting her phone down. "It'll be about an hour. They must be slammed by the after-church crowd."

"And this is the last week you're missing, right?" Mom asked.

"We've been there every Sunday except today and the day after we married. We're not skipping out often."

"I know. I just know you didn't go often while you were in medical school."

"Half the time I was working Sundays or late on Saturday. I promise, I'm not having a crisis of faith. I'll be there next week, unless I'm delivering a baby or something. Sometimes my work has to come first."

Mom nodded. "I just worry with Nate working on the house on the weekends that you won't go to church on your own."

"Nate has no intention of missing church either. Stop worrying so much!"

Mom smiled sheepishly. "You are my baby, you know."

"I know. And I love you for worrying."

"Are you going to be getting a new car soon?" Mom asked.

"Tomorrow," Shelby answered.

"Are you being facetious?"

"Nope. Nate and I talked about it last night. We're going to go look at vehicles after work tomorrow."

"Good. I'm tired of you driving that car that looks like it's going to die at any second."

"I'm fine, Mom. I promise." Shelby smiled. "Besides, I carry extra magnets in my glove box."

"What do you do with those?" Mom asked, her brows furrowed.

"I keep them just in case something falls apart and needs a magnet to pull it back together of course."

The other women laughed, but Mom backed off.

"What's next?" Tricia asked.

"Umm...I want to take one of the rooms down here as a home office, and we can unpack my medical books there," Shelby said. "I know Nate is taking the front room, but I can take the one beside it."

"Why not just share an office?" Mom asked.

"I think it's probably better if we have separate ones," Shelby replied. "When I need to look something up or study something, I want to be alone in absolute quiet."

"What will Nate do in his office?" Mom asked.

"He has a degree in accounting, and I know he works on his business dealings at home. He writes invoices and balances his checkbook. We both own businesses, and we need to do some work at home."

"I didn't realize Nate was that hands on with his family business."

"Trust me. He knows everything that's going on at any given time." Shelby found some plates and set the table. "We'll be ready when the food gets here."

As soon as the table was set, they went into the room she'd claimed for her office. There were some built-in shelves, and even a built-in desk. "This will be perfect for me."

While the others unpacked most of the boxes, Shelby unpacked her boxes of books, needing to know where each one had ended up.

When the doorbell rang, signaling the arrival of their lunch, Shelby all but ran to the door. Food. They all needed food.

Chapter Ten

The house was livable by late that night, and after work the following day, Nate arrived at Shelby's office to take her car shopping. She followed him to the car lot of his choice and they spent some time looking around at vehicles before they talked to a salesperson.

The girl selling the car was happy to answer all their questions, and she went on a test drive with them, showing them all the special features of the vehicle. They went home with a Chevy Equinox, and left Shelby's old car with them. They'd gotten very little as a trade-in, but neither of them cared. The car was off their hands.

After arriving home, they decided they needed one more night of DoorDash because neither of them felt up to cooking. "Wait!" Shelby said after they'd started talking about where to order from. "Tricia was here. Let me see if she left something in the oven for us."

She hurried into the kitchen, finding everything had been scrubbed clean. She didn't know if boxes had been unpacked, but the kitchen gleaming made her not care too terribly much. Opening the oven, she smiled. "We have supper!"

Nate followed her into the kitchen. "What did she make?"

"Pork chops, baked potatoes, and what looks like broccoli covered with cheese."

"Perfect," he said, reaching for an oven mitt. Sticking his hand into the oven, he pulled everything out. "It's all still hot too."

"Let's eat," she said, happy they wouldn't be ordering in again. She firmly believed that whatever you made at home was healthier than what you ate out.

She got them each a cold glass of water and carried it to the table. He'd already put plates on along with silverware and was carrying the food from the oven into the dining room.

"This looks amazing," she said.

He nodded. "I want to keep Tricia around for as long as possible. How many days is she working this week?" he asked.

"I have her working all five days. She's unpacking boxes as well as cleaning. I hope that's all right. I know I should have discussed it with you first."

He shook his head. "No, I think that's fine. It'll help us settle in here faster. It's hard enough living in a construction zone. Thanks for being so easy-going about it," he said.

"I get to be with you, so the house doesn't matter all that much. I only want to have a permanent home for when we're raising children. I don't think they should have to change schools often. Neither of us did."

"I understand that completely," he told her. His mind was back on when she'd stopped returning his calls. "You act like being with me is the most important thing for you, but you stopped returning my calls all those years ago. I still don't understand why."

She gaped at him for a moment, laying down her fork. "I didn't stop returning your calls. You stopped calling."

He shook his head. "I called every night at seven like you asked me to do. And you never called me back, even though I left a message with your roommate every night."

She thought back to her sophomore year and the first semester. "That's when I was rooming with Laura."

He nodded. "Yeah, I felt like I had a relationship with Laura and not you."

She shook her head. "Laura ended up being a terrible roommate. She stole from me. She never wrote down messages. She even took my car once in the middle of the night because hers was out of gas, and she didn't come back for three days."

His brows drew together, and he frowned. "But when you came back for Christmas, you didn't call."

"Because I'd waited by the phone for you all semester." Her eyes grew wide. "She was forwarding all calls to her phone. That must be what happened. I know Mom kept missing me when she called as well."

"And you didn't call me because I didn't call you." He frowned. "All these years, I thought you grew tired of me and quit returning my calls. I've always wondered what I did wrong."

"I've done the same thing. I decided that you never really cared for me if you couldn't last in a long-distance relationship with me for longer than you had. I quit coming back for breaks because it hurt too much to even be in the same town with you. I only came back after medical school because Mom kept begging. She wanted her whole family together. I don't think she was really all that worried about Aunt Lydia. She just wanted me home."

"I've been blaming you all this time. And feeling like I couldn't trust you."

She sighed. "I have been blaming you. I couldn't figure out why you were so fickle."

He closed his eyes for a moment, before reaching for her hand. "Let's never let things fester between us again. I've loved you since we were in ninth grade, and I've been afraid to trust you with my heart since you walked down the aisle toward me."

"Me too," she said in a whisper. "I love you, Nate. So very much."

"We're not going to let idiots come between us again," he said. "I can't believe we wasted so much time because of your stupid roommate."

"I should have guessed. She was so terrible, but it never occurred to me that you were still calling every night when the phone never rang. She was probably in a bar every time you called."

They finished their meal, and he sent her upstairs for a bath while he took care of the dishes. When he finished, he went up the stairs as well, stepping into the bathroom and stripping out of his clothes. "Hi you," he said softly, his heart feeling so full knowing what had really happened between them.

"Hi," she said. She still felt as if she'd done something wrong, and she needed to apologize. "All that time I've been blaming you, and I should have guessed what had happened because I was the one who lived with Laura."

He shook his head. "Don't blame yourself." He got into the tub, sitting beside her in the giant bath. "We could both feel guilty til the end of time, and it would change nothing."

She rested her head against his shoulder. "You forgive me then?"

"There's nothing to forgive. We were kept apart by a terrible roommate and life. Now we're together again, and everything is going to be perfect between us." He cupped her face in his hands, leaning down to brush a kiss across her lips. "It's all forgotten."

She wrapped her arms around his neck and pulled him down for a deeper kiss. "I promise to let you know if I feel something is wrong between us, and we'll talk it out. We should have talked about all this on our wedding day."

He shook his head adamantly. "I finally had you in my arms, and there was no way I was going to let you postpone the wedding night over something like this."

She laughed. "I didn't want to postpone the wedding night any more than you did. I'd planned to ask for a couple of months to get to know the man I married, but when I knew it was you, I was ready to strip and get on with it."

He chuckled. "And you really never even dated anyone else?"

She shook her head. "I'd look at someone and compare him to you, and I knew I'd never be able to look at him favorably after that. And I really did devote every minute to my studies."

"But we're good now, right?"

She nodded emphatically, tears in her eyes. "We are so good."

His hand covered her breast. "I kind of like how you feel with water all over you."

She laughed, moving her hand to his chest. "Ditto."

"Let's get out of here before we splash water all over this brand new floor."

She didn't have to be asked twice, standing up, she climbed over him and got out of the tub. Looking back over her shoulder, she asked, "Aren't you coming?"

Tossing him a towel, she dried off with another and moved toward the bed. There was no reason for any pretty sleepwear that night, because she knew her husband well enough to know he'd take it right off her.

SHELBY FELT THAT EVERYTHING was rather perfect the next day, and her nurses noticed as well as her sister. "What's gotten into you?" Rachel asked. "Well, other than Nate of course."

Shelby shook her head. "I'm in love with the man I'm married to. Who could ask for anything more from life?"

"Not me," Rachel said. "Andrew makes me feel the same way."

"As he should."

"That reminds me," Rachel said. "I think I might be pregnant. You want to test me?"

Shelby frowned. "I can test you, but I'm referring you to an OB. I'm not delivering any babies for anyone in my family!"

Rachel nodded. "Let me get you a sample."

Instead of getting one test out, Shelby grabbed two, deciding to test herself as well. Why not? She'd been married for over a month, and it wasn't like they hadn't been practicing their baby-making skills very frequently.

She ran a sample of her own at the same time as she ran Rachel's, putting an R on Rachel's and an S on her own.

She waited the three minutes and looked. Stunned at the results, she went into the reception area, and sat down beside her sister. "Wouldn't it be fun to have cousins born about the same time?" she whispered.

Rachel turned to her and squealed. "Both of us?"

Shelby nodded emphatically. "Both of us. We'll have to invite ourselves to Mom's for supper on Sunday, and we'll tell her at the same time. Can you stay quiet til then?"

"I have to tell Andrew," Rachel said.

"And I have to tell Nate. Just no one else. Not even Angela!"

Rachel stuck out her finger for a pinky swear, something the girls had done often when they were younger.

There was a patient at the window frowning at them when they looked up. Shelby laughed. "Sorry, my sister and I were just reminiscing a bit."

The woman laughed. "No problem. I know what it's like to have sisters."

As Shelby returned to the back for the next patient, she couldn't help but think about the baby growing inside her. A baby of hers and Nate's created with all the love they had inside them.

When Shelby got home that evening, Nate was already there and putting supper on the table. "Thank God for Tricia," he said as he looked at her.

Shelby knew she shouldn't tell him so quickly, and she should set up a special occasion meal or something before she told him, but she couldn't help herself. Walking into his arms, she kissed him. "I have some news..."

He frowned. "News? Don't tell me you found your dream house and you want to move again!"

She laughed. "Nothing like that." She took a deep breath as she looked up into his eyes. "I'm pregnant."

He stood for a moment, staring at her. "Seriously?"

She nodded, so excited she was ready to burst. He sat down in the chair behind him. "Seriously. I can't quite believe it, but I had all the signs, so I did a test at work today, and I am. But we can't tell anyone til Sunday."

"But I have to tell my mom."

Shelby shook her head. "No, not til after Sunday dinner at my Mom's."

"Why does your mom get to know first?" he asked. He genuinely didn't understand what was happening.

"It's just a promise Rachel and I made together. Please?"

"All right. It won't hurt anything to wait a few days before we tell her and make her the happiest woman alive."

"She's been waiting for grandkids since we were in high school! I think that's why she always let us study with your bedroom door closed."

He chuckled. "I think so too."

"My mom was a little more careful with us."

"Yeah, your door had to be open at least six inches if we were in there together. No one quite understood that we were putting the brakes on ourselves back then." He kissed her quickly. "So glad that's all over."

"Me too!" she said, looking at the table. "What did Tricia make for us?"

"Some sort of casserole. I've quit leaving a recipe for her, and just let her come up with stuff. She's learned enough about us now that it's not a big deal for her to just choose something."

"I agree." Shelby sat down at the table he'd already set. "I'm going to feed my baby for the first time knowing I was eating for two. It's silly how much that excites me."

"Will it hurt if we..."

She shook her head. "Not with a healthy pregnancy. We'll do just fine."

"Oh, good. I'm not ready to stop playing with my new toy yet."

She grinned. "And I'm not ready to stop playing with mine."

RACHEL AND SHELBY WAITED until after the prayer at Sunday dinner. Then they looked at their mother and said together, "We're both pregnant!"

Andrew was surprised about Shelby, and Nate was astonished about Rachel, but both men laughed. "I knew you weren't telling me everything," Nate said.

Mom sat stunned for a moment. "You're due close together?" she asked Rachel and Shelby.

Shelby answered. "About a week apart."

"That's enough for me to retire and take care of grandbabies full-time."

"I have an office attached to mine that I'm going to turn into a nursery," Shelby said. "Then we can have a nanny on the premises."

"Only if I get to be that nanny." Mom looked over at Angela. "I'm going to have four grandbabies soon."

Angela laughed. "You sure are. I hope you're happy."

Mom's tears answered that question for them all.

Epilogue

It was late June of the next year when Shelby went into labor. Even as Nate was grabbing her suitcase and putting her into the car, she called her mother. "Mom, I'm on my way to the hospital."

It was just after three in the morning, but she'd promised to call as soon as she headed for the hospital.

Mom laughed. "I'm at the hospital with Rachel. You need to ask if they can put you in a room near hers. The next one over is empty."

Soon, Shelby was holding her newborn in her arms. "What should we call him?" she asked Nate. They'd been discussing names, but nothing had seemed quite right.

"What about Zachary Charles? After both of our dads."

"Perfect! And we can call him Zach. Now why didn't we figure that out six months ago?"

Nate shrugged, staring down at Shelby with the baby. "Have I told you yet today how much I love you?" he asked.

She smiled. "I love you right back."

Milton Keynes UK
Ingram Content Group UK Ltd.
UKHW040642050923
428087UK00001B/182